There was no mistaking the mutual desire, the tension arising between them.

Selena struggled to keep up with this newfound awareness. This was her coworker. A man known for his prowess with the ladies. She couldn't let her Cinderella moment delude her into thinking this was something more. Not that she wanted... something more.

She scoffed. "They're taken with my clothes. With how I look. How many of them would notice me or find me appealing if they saw me in my regular work gear?"

"I would." He cleared his throat and leaned to whisper in her ear. "I have."

Her mouth popped open and she put some distance between them. She would admit she liked being found desirable, but she couldn't get caught up. She was dealing with a man who had a PhD in flirting, and she reminded herself that Trent could be teasing her. He had the gift of gab...and a gifted tongue if the rumors were to be believed. A rumor she was now very interested in investigating for veracity.

"I don't know if I believe that..." She licked her lips and Trent's eyes followed the movement. Her body heated and she crossed her legs, resisting the urge to fan herself.

Dear Reader,

The inspiration for this Valentine's Day story started with a Twitter call from an editor. She was seeking a different take on the popular holiday, and that got the creative wheels in my head turning and Selena and Trent's story came to life.

Selena and Trent each had different reasons why they shied away from love and a day dedicated to love, so going on this journey with them was a lot of fun. I loved the chance to delve into their backstories and to show that sometimes the right person for you could be right next to you if you just open your eyes.

I love reading deep stories with a rom-com feel and this was my first attempt at writing one. I especially love stories with strong supporting characters, and that's what I hope you found with Pammie. If you enjoyed reading this cute tale with some feel-good moments, I would love to hear your thoughts. Please connect with me on Facebook or join my newsletter at michellelindorice.com.

Michelle

The Valentine's Do-Over

MICHELLE LINDO-RICE

HARLEQUIN

SPECIAL
EDITION

Recycling programs
for this product may
not exist in your area.

ISBN-13: 978-1-335-72446-5

The Valentine's Do-Over

Copyright © 2023 by Michelle Lindo-Rice

For questions and comments about the quality of this book, please contact us at CustomerService@Harlequin.com.

Harlequin Enterprises ULC
22 Adelaide St. West, 41st Floor
Toronto, Ontario M5H 4E3, Canada
www.Harlequin.com

Printed in U.S.A.

Michelle Lindo-Rice is a 2021 Emma Award winner and a 2021 Vivian Award finalist. Michelle enjoys reading and crafting fiction across genres. Originally from Jamaica, West Indies, she has earned degrees from New York University; SUNY at Stony Brook; Teachers College, Columbia University; and Argosy University; and has been an educator for over twenty years. She also writes as Zoey Marie Jackson.

Books by Michelle Lindo-Rice

Harlequin Special Edition

The Valentine's Do-Over

Seven Brides for Seven Brothers

Rivals at Love Creek
Cinderella's Last Stand

Visit the Author Profile page
at Harlequin.com for more titles.

I would like to dedicate this book to my friend Lea.
I am rooting for your second-chance love.
I also must acknowledge my husband, John,
who is my talk-through partner and who helped me
push through to get this book written. Thank you to
my sister, Sobi Burbano, and Fran Purnell:
my unofficial first-reads crew. Thank you to the
Harlequin Special Edition team—Gail Chasan,
Megan Broderick and others who helped to shape
the story into a much better read. And a big thank-you
to my wonderful agent, who has such a sweet spirit
and bright smile: Latoya Smith.

Chapter One

Fifty-five days.

Fifty-five days from now, on January 1, Selena Cartwright would be celebrating her two-year anniversary on the *Weeknights with Trent and Selena Show*. Fifty-five days until she would earn equal pay with her cohost. A right she had fought for, with Trent Moon's backing.

She fussed with her messy updo and smoothed her brown slacks, making sure not to trip over the large area rug as she exited her dressing room and made her way to the radio booth. Trent and the producer, Carla Smith-Jones, were already inside. She could see the whites of his capped teeth and ran her tongue over hers as a reflex action. She needed to get to the dentist and stop chewing on the fruit snacks she was never without—serving as her lunch and dinner on many occasions. Come to think of it, what she actually needed was to make time in her schedule to eat, splitting herself between the show and her private practice as a mental health therapist.

Carla waved her inside. "It's about time you got here."

Selena glanced at the Movado watch on her slender wrist, a gift that had outlived the boyfriend of two years who had given it to her. She had five minutes before they went live. The trip from the Gracie Square Hospital, a facility for psychiatric patients, to the studio on Varick Street had taken the cabdriver close to an hour instead of the usual thirty minutes.

She touched her bangs and responded to Carla. "There was a serious accident and the rain didn't help. I don't know how some people get their driver's license."

"That's why I don't drive in the city unless I have to," Trent said with a laugh. "I have serious road rage."

Most days Selena loved the hustle and bustle of New York City but days like today made her consider relocating to Westchester or Poughkeepsie. It had taken her stylist thirty-three minutes to get her droopy curls tamed into a respectable bun. Even though it was a radio station, Selena and Trent were recorded and their sessions posted on social media. Her hair had to be on point—always. She couldn't afford the sistas coming for her like they had done to Gabby Douglas years ago at the Olympics. Who cared that the young woman was a record-breaking gymnast if her hair wasn't snatched right? That had been a snarky discussion Selena had engaged in across the airwaves.

"Thanks to cabs and the subway, I don't need a license," Carla said, blinking in slow motion.

Was that a carpet on her eyes? Selena mused, regretting talking her boss into getting lash extensions. That fad wasn't for everyone.

Selena scooted her chair at the long white table and dug in her bag for her ginger mints. She took out five and slipped three to Trent, keeping two for herself. He gave her a thumbs-up before sliding one of the two granola bars by his notepad over to her side.

"Thanks." She tore the bar open then stretched her legs.

Her black kitten pumps touched Trent's sneakers. He was dressed in black jeans and a hoodie with the words *I Can't Breathe* imprinted in white. Trent was passionate about using his celebrity status as a radio host to shed light on injustice. When she was still a listener, Trent had been one of the first people to interview Colin Kaepernick, the football player who had taken a knee during the national anthem in 2016 and had started a movement.

That was one of the reasons Selena had slashed her private practice hours to part-time and accepted Trent's offer to cohost. She admired his grit and, though he had the reputation of being a ladies' man, his integrity. Her move from an impulsive caller giving expert advice to sitting three feet across from him had been surreal. An experience far more rewarding than she could have ever imagined.

"Sorry," she mumbled, taking another bite of her bar.

"That's okay. It's not your fault you're freakishly tall." He chuckled, tapping long fingers on the table. She could see he was getting a kick out of messing with her, as usual.

"Don't blame me that you're just plain old average," she countered. He was an inch shy of six feet, and two inches taller than she was.

"If you really knew me, you'd take that back," he said, waggling his brows and running an index finger across his chin. A signature move that the women found appealing judging by the comments on their social media posts. That, along with his square jaw, brown skin and bedroom-bass voice. Their words, not hers.

"I see you forgot to leave your ego in your dressing room," Selena teased, sliding her gaze away from those honey-brown eyes.

"It's my backpack. I take it everywhere I go," he shot back.

She laughed, enjoying their verbal sparring.

"Save all that love for the air." Carla butted in before gesturing to the rest of the staff that they were going live in two minutes.

Selena and Trent had a great working relationship.

They admired and respected each other as colleagues and, because of that, their ratings had grown each quarter. Viewers enjoyed their banter and comradery. She was the more serious of the two, but Trent's passion and lightheartedness made for a nice balance on the show.

Only to herself would she admit his fineness. She had told Trent he was a broken-down version of Kofi Siriboe, but what she hadn't said was how Kofi was her man crush. Or rather, her boy toy. Her best friend, Nadine, had called Selena a cradle robber when she'd caught Selena ogling the actor from *Queen Sugar*. Nadine hadn't missed the physical similarities between the actor and Trent, pointing that out to Selena. Besides the fact that she didn't poop where she ate, Trent reminded her too much of her father. A father who'd called her mother, Helen, his number one...of many. Too many. A father who, when he'd left, had left her mother broken. And Helen was never the same.

So, Selena avoided charismatic men like Trent.

Calm. Safe. Borderline boring. That was her speed.

Glancing at her watch, she finished eating. Soon after, an intern brought them two bottles of water at room temperature, along with napkins. Taking a few sips, Selena wiped her mouth and then reapplied her nude lipstick.

Carla gave them a quick signal before scurrying into the sound booth. She was in her late forties, trim, and moved like she was on a catwalk. Outfitted in an A-line dress and high boots, Selena thought her producer looked confident and gorgeous, especially with her silver-gray hair in a pixie cut.

Selena felt pride in knowing she had contributed to the other woman's aura and wellness. A few months ago, Carla had been going through a nasty divorce so Selena had offered her confidential sessions. Then, to avoid a conflict of interest, she had referred Carla to another therapist.

Carla spoke through the intercom. "We're going live in ten…nine…"

Selena straightened as her heart rate accelerated. The anticipation of reaching out to people would never grow old.

From under his lashes, Trent studied his cohost, admiring her cream tank top and brown pantsuit. Her signature color scheme. She had completed her look with chunky gold accessories and light makeup. Even her lipstick was a glossy shade of brown. Selena tended to favor muted tones, something he believed she had adopted as a therapist. Trent found her style classy. She had told him once she didn't want to be sexualized. Or had she mentioned it on air? He couldn't remember, but with those high cheekbones, full lips, thick lashes and generous curves, there was no disguising her beauty.

She didn't know it, but his friends James and Dontae had ragged on him for weeks, begging for introductions once they had seen how fine she was. A request Trent had denied. He liked to keep his professional and personal lives separate. In their twenty-two months together, his interactions with his cohost were limited to their airtime and planning for the next day.

He heard the countdown signaling that they were about to go on air and cleared his throat. Then he greeted their listeners and gave an update on the weather before jumping into their first segment.

"It's time for us to *Listen to Our Listeners*," he said and waited as Carla cued the intro.

Once Selena had joined the show, their audience had begun sending emails and letters seeking advice, and their ratings had blown up. To handle the large influx of communication, their assistants read most of the mail and provided Trent and Selena with five letters each to read. They would then choose one or two to share during the show and offer suggestions. Listeners would also call in and express their thoughts. The segment was a huge success.

Carla had already tossed around the idea of expanding their hour to ninety minutes. That's why he had pushed for Selena to receive equal pay though she didn't have the ten years' on-air experience he had.

Selena chimed in. "I have a letter from a listener who calls herself 'A Crying Heart.'"

Trent tensed with the memory of the powerful visual imagery in the letter. Selena believed an English major had penned the words. Trent had pushed for Selena to read it, though his cohost had felt it too personal. After muting his microphone, he picked up one of the ginger mints, unwrapped it and plopped it into his mouth. He closed his eyes, savoring the strong sensation and listening to Selena's singsong voice, which depicted her Jamaican heritage. She had migrated to America at ten years old and, though she was a naturalized citizen, had maintained her accent and culture.

Selena moved closer to her microphone and began to read, and he felt everything around him still.

> "'Every year about this time, a sense of dread begins to fill my being. All around me, there is a beauty that comes from the colorful foliage. Families unite over steaming mugs of trendy themed coffees and engage in social activities meant to bring them closer together; end the year with goodwill. I move with the bustle of the crowd, smiling at the appropriate time, voicing the right sentiment, but on the inside, I am withering, dying like a tree left bare after shedding its leaves. I feel alone.'"

His heart squeezed even though he knew the contents of the letter. Hearing the words read aloud evoked strong emotions. Selena's intonation moved him and their listeners were responding, judging by the flashing phone lines.

Selena took a sip of water and continued.

"'For the first time this year, I don't want to pretend. I want to wallow, submerge myself until I am overwhelmed under the grief of being alone especially with Valentine's Day coming in about three months. The worst holiday of all because it beams on me with the brightness of the sun and I am left alone under the heat of the spotlight, shouting my singleness. My heart aches as I wait for spring and the end to all this madness, where for a few months I can embrace being all right with myself. But until then, my heart bleeds.'
"Signed, 'A Crying Heart.'"

Selena reached for the box of tissues and dabbed her eyes.

Trent swallowed the last of his mint and turned on his microphone. In a subdued tone, he said, "Wow. I felt every nuance in each word. A Crying Heart, we hear you and thank you for sharing your most intimate thoughts with us. I found your letter honest and raw. How about we take our first caller to get some listener feedback?" He pressed one of the open lines and smiled at Selena, who was giving him a look of gratitude. Her cheeks were a little flushed and her lashes spiky. *I got you*, he mouthed.

"Hello? Am I on the air?" a woman asked. Her voice cracked and she sniffled.

"Yes, you're live with Trent and Selena," Selena said in a calm tone.

Trent admired her professionalism. He focused on the caller.

"I want to say that I'm glad A Crying Heart had the courage to write what I've been feeling all these years. I'm happily single and it's awful that I have to endure my family asking me when I'm going to find someone, giving me looks of pity. Like I'm good for the most part. Except when Valentine's Day comes around, slapping me in my face. I know that February 14 is all about love but I hate that day with a passion."

He gave a small chuckle of understanding. "Imagine the irony of hating a day that is supposed to be about love."

"I know," the caller breathed. "I feel guilty but I absolutely despise it. It feels so good to admit this to someone."

"Thank you so much for sharing," Selena said before taking another caller.

This time it was a young man. "Yo, tell me why, I'm so glad I was turning the dial and heard this. Cuz I'm good, too. My mother is on me to give her a grandchild. But I want to travel. I want to do things."

And the calls continued.

"I hate being single," someone said. "I buy myself flowers and chocolates so I don't feel so pitiful."

"I don't like being alone," another voiced.

"I hate it."

"I think Valentine's all about commercialism."

The comments kept coming. They spent the rest of the hour taking calls, moving with the flow. Trent and Selena could hardly keep up with the outpour and they tabled their talk on pumpkin spice. She had reached into her bag for her phone and had read some of their social media comments.

"A Crying Heart, you started something tonight," Trent said once they were at the end. "Let's keep this conversation going. Please send us your comments and stories using the hashtag ValentineSingle and we will continue this tomorrow."

"Thanks for tuning in with us tonight and until then—"

Selena surprised him when she interrupted with, "A Crying Heart, I hope you call in tomorrow before the weekend. I'd love to talk to you because I, too, hate Valentine's Day."

His mouth dropped. In slow motion. The holidays brought their biggest sponsors. He avoided looking into the booth, knowing Carla was probably about to pass out. Selena slipped back into her chair with a huge grin on her face, like she didn't know what she had just done.

Trent evoked every ounce of experience he possessed to keep from stammering through the signature slogan. "Keep your dreams sweet and your hope strong. Good night." He disconnected his microphone and looked at the woman he had always seen as constant. The woman who sat with her arms folded, holding an expression similar to Angela Bassett's after setting a car on fire in the blockbuster classic *Waiting to Exhale*. Then he asked, "What did you just do?"

Chapter Two

This wasn't a "what" question. The real question was *why*.

Carla rushed into the room, her eyes wide and her mouth rounded like a puffer fish. "Do you know what you've just done?" she sputtered.

Selena stood, knots the size of brambles whirling in her stomach. "I—I don't know what came over me. I don't even know why I said that." Well, she had a good idea, but it wasn't one she would share. Every time she left after a visit with her mother, it stirred her emotions.

"We might lose some of our biggest investors because of this," Carla said, running a hand through her short strands and drawing raspy breaths. "Saying you hate Valentine's Day when we have commercials from contributors like Hershey's and Dunkin' Donuts could be catastrophic. Give me some time to strategize and we can talk tomorrow after the show."

The trio parted ways. During the cab ride home, Selena replayed Carla's parting words.

It rattled her to see the other woman's composure slip. Before her on air confession, Selena had been looking forward to binge watching Season 4 of *The Crown on Netflix*. She had finally started the series and had planned to catch a couple episodes. But Selena didn't turn on the television. She hadn't been able to concentrate.

Her upcoming conversation with Carla preoccupied most of her thoughts the rest of the night and throughout the day. When she entered the studio that Thursday night, Trent tried to reassure but all she could think about was how she might lose her job because of her loose tongue.

An image of her mother, Helen, in her room at the psychiatric hospital flashed before Selena. She tightened her lips. Love had shredded Helen's heart and mind since Selena was a teen. She shuddered on the inside. After seeing her mother in that state, she had sworn off love. For life. However, she knew better than to voice her real feelings on the air. Like Carla said, they had sponsors.

She made it through the show on auto pilot, but the minute it concluded, Selena cornered Carla and apologized.

"I'm sorry. I didn't think what I said was harmful."

"You didn't think. Period," Carla snapped. "In today's time, words have an impact. One statement could haunt you forever and be the end of your career. Which could potentially affect other people's livelihood. Mine included."

Selena's heart pounded, her guilt intensifying, even though she suspected Carla was exaggerating a bit.

Trent came over to where they were huddled, his phone in hand. "I've got a confession to make. I hate Valentine's Day, too." He released a breath, like he'd admitted something horrible. "That felt good to say," he said with a small chuckle.

Carla flailed her hands. "This is not the time for humor. I don't think you'd be laughing when we're out of a paycheck."

"I wasn't trying to be funny," Trent said, "I'm being honest and you're being melodramatic."

Selena caught his eye. "You don't have to defend me, Trent, by saying that. I know I messed up big-time." She faced Carla. "Maybe I can tweet an apology."

"At this point, our public relations team has advised that we do nothing and ride this out." Carla warned. Her phone buzzed. After reading the notification, she held up a hand. "I'm going to need you both to sit tight. The producer for the next show just called out and they need me to step in. I shouldn't be long." She flounced out the room.

Knowing that Carla's wait time could be anywhere

from several minutes to an hour, Selena retrieved her laptop to work on client notes. During that time, Trent either napped or scrolled through his phone.

"I'm getting hungry," Selena said about forty minutes later. "What about you?"

Trent nodded but she wasn't sure if he had registered her words. His head popped up just as Carla returned. He held up his phone. "You've got to see this. We currently have over 100,000 views."

Her mouth dropped. "Are you serious?"

"Take a look for yourself if you don't believe me. Hashtag ValentineSingle is trending." His eyes were bright. "You're a sensation, Selena."

"What?" Selena shook her head. "I don't understand." She had been busy with clients most of the day and had avoided social media on purpose.

"We're not going to lose sponsors," Trent said with much fascination as he continued to read. "We're going to gain some."

"Let me see that," Carla said, snatching the phone. As she scanned the contents, her worried lines disappeared and soon she began to chuckle. "Oh, snap. What have you started? This is genius." Handing Trent his phone, she tapped her chin. "I think we can play this to our advantage."

Selena sagged, biting on her lip to keep from smiling. It was funny how quickly Carla's demeanor had changed.

"Somebody's going to remix this and make a song out of it," Trent said.

Selena raced to get her own phone. A few clicks

later, she was on her social media page. Then she pulled up a short clip from their segment and pressed play. Sure enough, there she was, on repeat, saying, "I, too, hate Valentine's Day." She groaned at her red cheeks and puffy face, but played it again. "This is bananas," she muttered.

"No," Carla corrected, rubbing her hands, "this is an opportunity. And when it knocks, we've got to answer the door." She scurried over to the table and sat in her usual position at the head. "Pull up a seat, guys. It's time we strategize. Let's pounce on this."

Trent looked at his watch. "Let me make a quick call. I'll be back."

Selena watched him retreat, then eyed the clock and slipped into her chair. It was almost eight thirty. Judging by the excitement on Carla's face, they could be there for another two hours. But considering minutes ago, she had been worried about losing her job, Selena wasn't complaining.

"Let's order dinner," Carla said, pressing the intercom, most likely to call her assistant. "What do you want? Is Chinese good?"

"Yes, Chinese is fine. I'll nibble on whatever you get," Selena said, scrunching her nose. She could never decide on what she wanted to eat when she remembered to eat.

"I'll get a little of everything."

When her assistant didn't answer, Carla left the room.

Selena wasn't a cook. In Helen's lucid days, her mother had tried to teach her, but without any success. Selena had burned water. Yes, water. Granted, she had been working on a paper at the time. But still. Helen had given up on cooking lessons after that. Then her bestie, Nadine, had tried to teach her how to make some simple survival meals, but Selena cut her thumb and had needed stitches. Selena avoided the kitchen after that, hating how she had failed.

Once she had graduated from Howard University and moved into her own place, Selena usually kept her freezer stacked with frozen dinners. A month ago, she had started using a meal prep program and enjoyed having healthy meals without the labor— but she kept forgetting to place her orders online and was too busy to schedule one-on-one consultations with the chef.

Trent returned and sunk into the chair across from her. "What did I miss?" His tone sounded lackluster and his brown eyes held worry.

"Not much. Carla's ordering dinner. Everything all right with you?" Selena asked.

He nodded and hunched his shoulders, signs he was far from okay. Selena found herself filled with concern at his lack of joviality.

"You want to talk about it?" She'd cocked her head and asked in a low tone in case Carla was in the sound booth.

Trent looked at her. Really looked at her. Like he had never seen her before. She squirmed under his intense scrutiny and raised a brow. He opened his mouth, like he wanted to say something, before shaking his head. "Nah. I'm good. How about you tell me why you hate Valentine's Day?"

Trent watched as Selena broke eye contact and lowered her gaze. Her long lashes fanned her cheeks. "I don't like to talk about it." She drummed her fingers on the tabletop.

After he had gotten off the phone with his sister Pammie, short for Pamala, Trent had been torn, feeling guilty. He was happy Mindy, her caretaker, had been available to stay later. But Pammie had wanted him to come home and keep his promise to make ice cream sundaes. She hadn't understood that he needed to work. He hated hearing her cry, found it hard to handle her disappointment. Fortunately, Mindy had bribed her with Oreo cookies and Trent had gotten an "I love you" before the call ended.

So, yes, he had been agitated when he'd reentered the room. For a second, he had wanted to confide in Selena. But he meant to stay in the lane called business. He wouldn't cross the line into personal. There was a big difference between being personable and getting personal.

He focused on the painting of the waves behind her and changed the topic, turning the attention off himself.

"Really?" he snorted. "You don't want to talk about it? You'll have to, because you opened the door to that story when you blurted out how you despised Valentine's Day." He exaggerated to jolt her into opening up. He had never seen Selena lose her cool stance and he was intrigued. For the first time since they had started working together, he wondered about her. Her backstory. He wanted to know more than just her profession and that she was a great work partner. He wanted to know what made her…human. Flawed. Like the rest of the world. Like him.

"Despise? That's a strong word." She licked her lips before she gave him a challenging look. "How about you go first? Were you kidding when you said you didn't like the holiday?"

He rubbed his chin and debated whether to answer. It was something he did when he was nervous or in deep thought, a habit he had picked up from his dad. "I don't know if I can trust you with the story of the biggest humiliation of my life."

Her eyes flashed and she scooted her chair around the table next to his. "Now you have to tell me. I'm going to bug you until you fess up." A whiff of jasmine teased his nose. It was light, airy, like the woman next to him.

"You have to promise not to tell."

She slapped his arm. "The fact that you have to ask is insulting. I'm a therapist and I know all about confidentiality."

"Yeah, but I'm not a patient," he said, stalling. He was going to stretch this conversation as long as he could.

"Yes, but I'm a friend."

With a jolt, Trent accepted she was right. She was a friend. Of sorts. He knew he could trust her. He knew he liked her personality. He dropped his voice to a whisper. "All right, bet. I'm a tell you but you have to swear on your pinky toe that you will never tell another living soul."

"My pinky toe?" she asked, cracking up. "Trent, you're so silly, but I promise you on my pinky toe."

"Let me see it," he teased, giving her a light shove on the shoulder.

She pursed her lips. "You play too much. My feet have been in these shoes for hours. I can't take off my shoes."

"I guess you don't want to know then." He shrugged.

They squared off. After a moment's hesitation, Selena took off her shoe—size nine, if he had to guess—and lifted her foot.

"You sure are nosy," he teased.

"You best believe it." She wiggled her foot back into her pump, leaning into him for support. "Now, tell me."

Carla came back into the room, diverting their attention from their current conversation. "Dinner will be here in fifteen minutes." She looked ready to jump and touch the roof. "I've got some great news. Unbelievable, really."

"Share it, then," Trent said.

Selena used that opportunity to scoot back to her usual side of the table.

"A sponsor called to double their advertisement

time slots. The higher-ups are on fire. They are even thinking of expanding the show into a two-hour segment."

"Say what?" Selena yelled. "That's amazing. Wow."

Trent's stomach clenched. Both women had their eyes on him, waiting for him to display his excitement.

He worked hard to appear relaxed and easygoing. But he had a regimented daily schedule. Had to. Ever since he had become his younger sister's guardian, Trent had made huge changes to his lifestyle. Gone was the bachelor filling his nights with one of the many swarming beauties around him. If he wasn't working or at the gym, he was with Pammie.

But Friday and Saturday nights were his time to hang with the boys or treat a woman to a five-star night in a hotel. He never took the ladies home and he paid Mindy double to take care of Pammie. But that was built into his sister's routine. She was used to it.

Trent hoped Pammie would adjust to his expanded work hours as this would disrupt her routine.

"Well, it's just talks for now. But let's ride this wave until our butts slide across the sand," Carla said. "So, tomorrow's show, we'll make another call for Bleeding Heart—"

"You mean A Crying Heart," Trent corrected.

"Yes, or whatever she calls herself," Carla said with a wave of her hand. "We'll see if she calls in. I think we should begin the show by making the plea, and with Selena telling why she hates Valentine's Day so much, and then, Trent, you'll share your story."

"What?" Trent shook his head. "I didn't announce that on the air. I don't want to tear open that can of humiliation for all to see."

"You can and you will," Carla said in that tone she used when she didn't want an argument. "I spoke with the execs and, it was only because I told them that their superstar—sorry, Selena—felt the same way, that they decided to get on board."

Trent dug his shoes into the floor to keep from yelling. He was shocked to discover he didn't like surprises. Well, he did. But not the kind that interfered with his schedule.

"I'll share my reason," Selena said in a low voice. She sounded like the proverbial sacrificial lamb. He couldn't let his partner put herself out there and not do the same.

"Fine," he growled. "Tomorrow, I'll tell my tale."

"Just remember we have children listening," Carla advised, eyeing them both with caution, before continuing. "Once you're both done baring your souls, we'll take more callers and read another letter or two from the massive number of emails." She pinned her gaze to the ceiling before looking at them. "Then we'll end the night with a bang and usher in the weekend on a high note. Got any ideas?"

As if on cue, the intern came in with paper products, utensils, and containers with a variety of dishes. Trent's stomach growled and his mouth watered. He had leftover steak and potatoes at home, but the sandwich he'd had for lunch and the granola bar snack had worn off. He grabbed a paper plate and added rice, chicken with broccoli and an egg roll. Selena packed her plate with a tiny spoonful of everything.

While they were eating, Selena dropped her fork and snapped her fingers. "I got it. We need to have our very own Valentine's celebration. Like maybe a dance."

Carla cocked her head. "A dance?"

"How will that help?" Trent asked.

Selena picked up her fork and twirled lo mein noodles around it. "Let me explain. We need to honor singles. Give all the couples in love the proverbial cut of the eyes. We need to throw a Valentine's Day dance. But for singles only. No couples allowed."

Chapter Three

She could smell the curry as soon as she entered the door of her best friend's third-floor studio apartment in Brooklyn Heights. Nadine had moved here two years ago because of its proximity to the NYU Langone medical center where she worked as an ER nurse.

"I can't believe you're cooking at midnight," Selena said, hanging her rain jacket on the hook behind the front door and wiping her feet on the mat with the words Did You Call First?. The kitchen was to the immediate right, with the bathroom steps away. Tucked in the furthest corner was the queen-sized bed on which they had shared many nights watching the television mounted on the huge half-wall. The wall divided the bedroom from the living room area, giving a small measure of privacy.

"If I don't cook now, I'll end up buying junk," Nadine said, giving her a hug before hastening over to the stove to stir the food. "I'm working a double tomorrow night, so I've got to be prepared." Nadine popped a small piece of meat in her mouth and wiggled her hips. "This curry chicken is giving me life right now. I put a pinch of Scotch bonnet pepper in there so that mild heat hits the back of your tongue just right."

Selena's mouth watered. Nadine was critical of her cooking, so if she was saying this was good, then the meal would be off the charts. Her tummy grumbled even though it was packed tighter than sardines in a can. "You know I'm taking a container home."

"I got you." Her friend gave a thumbs-up sign.

Placing her purse on the small dining table across from the kitchen, Selena massaged her neck, appreciating the stunning view of the Brooklyn Bridge at night. The bright lights drowned out the sounds of the city, the honking, and the squeals of the trains. That view was the second reason Nadine had chosen this spot, paying over two thousand dollars per month for a thousand square feet of living space. The third had to do with Nadine's unhealthy crush on Matt Damon, whom she had yet to run into by planned accident.

"I can't believe you dropped that bombshell on the air," Nadine said, her metal fork clinking against the stainless-steel everyday pan. The sound was the music that made Selena's stomach dance. Selena had bought her friend a set of Ironclad, knowing how much Nadine loved her pots.

"I didn't know you were listening in."

"I was working last night, but this morning Mommy sent me a clip of you saying you hate Valentine's Day. I texted you right away."

Nadine's parents had low-key adopted Selena as their child. The Johnsons had celebrated Selena's accomplishments more than her own mother had.

Selena smiled. "Yes, I got your freaked-out emojis but I had a strategy session with Carla and Trent. We're spinning this whole thing, which will build our brand, expand our hours, make a profit, and give our listeners a chance to party." She briefly outlined her idea of the singles dance, promising to share more details once she had them.

Selena stretched her neck and yawned.

"Girl, go sit down. You sound like a donkey braying," Nadine said with a laugh.

Forcing her tired feet to move toward the love seat, Selena sat and propped her legs on the wooden storage bin that doubled as a coffee table and footrest. "Give me a break. I spent hours in a meeting after work when I needed to be sleeping. At least they fed me." She closed her eyes.

"You're doing too much. You've got to choose between the practice or the show. The show might seem like a part time gig but the PR demands take up a lot of your time."

She felt weary to her bones. "I know. I know." She stifled a yawn. "But I like helping people."

"So, what about helping yourself? Self-care is important. You can't help people, if you're not around."

Nadine's solemn words sunk in. Selena popped one eye open. Before she could formulate a response, her mouth opened to form a huge yawn. Prying the other eye open, Selena pinned her gaze on her friend.

"You should have gone home instead of coming here. You plopped a fortune into that gorgeous mausoleum on the Upper West Side." Nadine shook her head. "I don't get why you bought that townhouse and then refuse to enjoy it."

Those words jolted her awake. "You know why. You made me buy that monstrosity because I was being featured in *Essence* magazine."

"Yes, we Jamaicans are coming up in life." Her eyes held compassion. "And it doesn't feel like home because you haven't made it one. Your walls are bare and your furnishings sparse. You need to put up pictures and add little knickknacks to make it yours." Nadine turned off the burner before washing her hands and wiping them with a paper towel. She then retrieved her containers. Knowing Nadine, she would have enough food for at least three days. Nadine always cooked too much and Selena's tummy reaped the rewards.

"What pictures?" Selena pointed to Nadine's family portrait where she stood between her two doting, smiling parents. "Not everyone has a mother like yours, who is willing to help you decorate. Or a father who will hang pictures twenty times if you ask." She spoke the words without envy. Since she had met Nadine in ninth grade at Jamaica High School seventeen years ago, she had fallen in love with her friend's petite parents. The three of them made her feel like a giant. They were small but their love was large.

"Boo-hoo. You can afford to hire someone and you do have pictures."

Her shoulders slumped, sinking her further into the love seat. For a beat, she watched Nadine's precise movements as she shared the steaming rice and chicken into the glass containers. Her friend didn't do plastic. It wasn't eco-friendly or healthy. Since her father's heart attack eighteen months ago, Nadine had vowed to change her lifestyle and had been urging Selena to do the same. Slow down.

Selena released a breath. "It's not the same."

Nadine dropped the spoon into the pan and placed a hand on her hip. "You can't press Pause. You can't keep your life in a freeze frame, waiting for Ms. Helen to turn back into the mother she once was. It's been twenty years. At some point…" She shook her head and stopped talking. Wiping her brow, she went back to her task.

Selena figured her friend was tired of repeating herself. They'd had variations of this conversation countless times. She sighed. "I can't give up on her."

Once she was finished with her meal prep, Nadine would wash all the dishes and clean her stove like Meena Johnson had instilled. Ms. Meena didn't play that. You didn't cook in or leave a dirty kitchen. Selena could hear Ms. Meena's voice in her head. *What if visitors drop by? What a big disgrace.*

Welp. That was one benefit of not cooking. Selena's kitchen was always clean. Pristine... Untouched.

Nadine put the pots in the sink and turned on the faucet. Then she continued. "I'm not asking you to give up on your mother, friend. I wouldn't ask you to do something I wouldn't do. I'm asking you to live. I'm asking you to take your life out of those storage bins and begin to celebrate your achievements. And, for goodness' sake, have some f-u-n. Do something unexpected."

Though it wasn't the first time she had heard them, those passionately uttered words struck Selena's heart with the force of a cannonball. She pictured the two large gray bins in her closet filled with pictures of her prom and her graduations, her sorority mementos and her awards. Everything was tucked away. Compartmentalized. Like her life.

Tears came to her eyes and she sniffled. "I went to see her today." She glanced at the sunflower clock. "Well, technically, it was yesterday. Mommy kept her back turned away from me. She refused to talk to me." Her breath hitched. "Said I looked like my father and cut her eyes at me. No matter how much I accomplish, I'll never be good enough. She'll never see me as something more. That's why I don't do love.

Look what it did to her. And, if I'm like him, what if I cause this pain on someone else?"

Leaving the pots to soak, Nadine came to sit next to her and opened her arms. Selena scooted low so she could rest her head on her much shorter friend's chest.

"Oh, honey. You're a therapist, so I know I'm preaching to the choir, but I'll say it anyway. You know your mother's sick. You can't take her words to heart." Nadine cradled her close.

"I know. That's exactly what I tell my patients." Selena squeezed out the words. Her chest felt constricted. "But this pain is something fierce and every time I think I have conquered it and put it to rest, it rears its head. She hates my father. What does that say about how she feels about me? She thinks I'm just like him though I haven't left her. I'm here." Her shoulders shook and the dam to her emotions burst. "I'm here. I'm here. I said that so many times, but she didn't want to hear it."

She felt Nadine stiffen beside her and steeled herself.

"You need to quit going to that facility. Your mother is gone. She's a shell of her former self. All she is now is bitter and all she does is injure you. A parent is supposed to heal not harm."

Selena straightened and grabbed a tissue from the napkin box on the floor. She wiped her face. "I'll be all right. I'm just in my feelings. I'll be back to myself in the morning."

Wiping her hands on her thighs, Nadine cupped Selena's cheeks. "I'll let it go, but I need you to know you're not your father. You would never desert your family like he did and especially how he did. If you are like him in any way, then you're the best of him."

All Selena could do was nod because she wasn't sure how much she believed her friend. But Nadine wasn't finished.

"There had to be something good about him or Ms. Helen would have never messed with that man in the first place much less married him. My friend, you're worthy of love and to be loved. Ms. Helen shunning you is her loss. You're a great friend, loyal, caring and kind."

Nadine lifted a finger with each point she made. "You're working hard to pay all your mother's expenses. She's well taken care of. You paid for my nursing school, you renovated my parents' house, and you surprised them with an all-inclusive package to Jamaica for Thanksgiving. They are way beyond ecstatic to return home and I'm sure that's all they will talk about for the next twelve days. Even though you didn't have to do anything because we love you. Period. You don't have to buy our love. You'll make a great wife and mother one day because you are not your past. So keep moving toward your future."

Selena squirmed. She didn't like when Nadine talked about what she had done for them. Gifting was her love language. She chuckled to lighten the air and to shift the conversation from her generosity. She also needed to skirt away from the dart that maybe she was trying to buy their love. "All this from the woman who is determined to be a serial dater and the life of the party until she's at least a hundred," she joked.

"You got that right." Nadine gyrated. "They don't make men like my daddy anymore. Love 'em and leave 'em. That's my motto. I bought the T-shirt, so it must be true."

She had indeed purchased a shirt with that slogan. In several colors.

"Yet you tell me to settle down? Can't you see how contradictory that is?"

"Because that's who you are. You've got to be true to you. If I am a serial dater, you're a serial monogamist."

"I've been single for a couple years. And you've never liked anybody I've dated."

"That's because you go for those boring men. Plaid shirts tucked into khaki pants."

Selena cracked up. "There's nothing wrong with a man wearing those clothes. You're a mess."

"There is if he has the belt buckled tight, showing an even smaller waist than mine."

"Whatever." Selena shook her head. "I can't with you."

Nadine cocked her head before changing topics. "Are you going to put your mother's business on the air?"

"Why not?" she shot back, her voice edged with bitterness. "It's not like she'll be tuning in anyway."

Nadine lifted a brow.

Selena rubbed her temples. "I know I sound… snarky. I only plan on telling how I feel about Valentine's Day from my viewpoint. What happened to my mother affected me. My childhood. I'm speaking from that perspective. That's my experience. My truth." She lowered her voice. "Get this, Trent's sharing, too. Turns out he's not too fond of the holiday, either."

Nadine's eyes went round. "What? Mr. Smooth Operator doesn't do Valentine's? That's hard to believe."

Selena nodded.

"Why, though? Did he tell you?"

She shook her head. "No. He's spilling the tea on tomorrow's show."

"Oh, you best believe I'll be tuning in. Me and the parents."

Trent stood by Pammie's bed, watching his sister's five-foot frame rise up and down while she slept. He reached down to take the JoJo Siwa bow out of her hair before pulling the pink unicorn covers up close to her chin. Then he smiled.

"I'm sorry I wasn't here to help you make sundaes. I'll make it up to you. I promise," he whispered before kissing her on the cheek. He could hardly believe she was twenty-one years old now. When his parents had brought her home, Trent had showered her face with kisses. Her tiny hand had wrapped around his hand and his heart. That had never changed. His sister had been born with Down's syndrome and, from the moment she'd arrived, Trent had been her protector. They had been inseparable until he'd left for Yale University. His parents had made him attend. Trent had been willing to turn down the full ride and commute to Queens College to stay close to Pammie. He would never forget her little body shaking as she'd sobbed when he had pulled out of the driveway to begin his journey to New Haven, Connecticut.

That's why he had moved Pammie in with him instead of placing her in a special home after their parents' deaths. Trent was grateful to be in a position where he could afford to provide her with the best.

Turning on the Disney night-light in case she had to use the bathroom during the night, Trent hoisted the giant unicorn off her bed and placed it in the corner of the room. Her pink bedroom was a blend of the child and woman that she was—featuring movie posters of her favorite films along with her stuffed unicorn collection.

His cell buzzed. It was Dontae.

Trent sped out of the room so he wouldn't disturb his sister and answered the phone. "What's up, man?"

"Yo, please tell me you're not about to do what I think you're about to do," Dontae said.

"I am. I'm laying it all out there tomorrow." He could hear the wind blowing in the background. Dontae must be calling from his truck.

"Bruh, don't go out like that, man," Dontae pleaded. "Don't do it. I was fixing a busted pipe when I got your text. Then I got an emergency call about a broken toilet or I would have called you sooner than this. But the entire time I was working, you were on my mind. I couldn't wait to call you. You know Renee and Keyshaun might be listening in. She don't need her head swole, thinking you still want her or something after all these years."

Trent gripped his iPhone at the mention of his ex-fiancé and ex-friend, and walked to his living room area. He sat into the U-shaped sectional and pulled the large ottoman into the space to close it in. "I'm over it. And her. This is about building the bank account. Adding more zeroes to my name."

"All right, man. That girl hurt you like nobody's business. She was wrong to the umpteenth power, on so many levels. I don't want you going down memory lane and getting all depressed again. Black men don't do therapy and this woman had you laid out on that couch for months."

"I did therapy. And I'm black. My parents died not too long after that, don't forget." Trent sighed. He hated talking about his parents' deaths. He didn't think he would ever get over losing them both in a car accident. He also hated how he sounded defensive about seeking much-needed help. "Don't feed into that stereotype. That's why so many of us are hurting and lashing out because we don't handle our pain the right way."

"Man, ease up with that. I didn't mean to get you started on that soapbox. You see how I handled my issues. My fists landed me behind bars. I lost my track scholarship because of all that nonsense. It was like I couldn't leave the hood behind. It's soaked deep in my DNA and though I'm proud of my heritage, I needed a better life. If it weren't for you, I'd be… I don't even know where I be right now. You know I'm just messing with you about that whole therapy thing. Truth is, I wish I'd had the guts to seek help when my brother got shot." He paused a beat.

Dontae had told Trent that he had been there to see his brother take his last breath. Shot because he had stolen a pack of gum from the corner store on a dare. A pack of gum. That stuff stayed with you for life.

"Yep. I needed to sprawl on somebody's couch," Dontae said. "Especially if my therapist had looked like yours. Cuz that lady was fine as all get-out."

The men shared a laugh. Trent didn't add that he'd asked her out after their sessions had ended, but Mariana Adams hadn't been about to break protocol and date her former client.

"But back to this whole Valentine's thing. Did you tell James yet?" Dontae asked.

Trent tensed. "No. Not yet."

"You'd better give him a heads-up. You know he's not above acting the fool. He might call the radio station. Or worse, go knock on Keyshaun's door." The background noise stilled and Trent heard a door slam, signaling Dontae was home.

"I'm counting on you keeping him cool."

James's temperament was suitable in his role as a

bouncer, but he could be a hothead when it came to his friends. A hothead with King Kong-sized fists. Add that to a Superman complex... Let's just say Trent had ended up pleading for Keyshaun's face— and life. Keyshaun's nose would be crooked as long as he stayed on this side of the earth, but according to James, Keyshaun should give thanks he was still breathing.

"I'm on it. I already plan to be there with him when you go live. We plan to listen in at Ms. Yancy's house."

"Good plan." The only person tougher than James was his mother. They had each felt the tip of her wooden spoon at some point. She wielded that thing with more skill than a Samurai.

"You sure you go'n do this?" Dontae asked again.

Trent wiped his brow. He didn't want to look like a chump but he didn't want Selena putting herself out there and not do the same. He released a huge breath of air. "I'm sure. Maybe it will help somebody."

Dontae snickered. "If telling yourself that helps you tell the tale, then all right."

Trent's phone buzzed. "Hang on. Let me check my cell real quick. I got a message."

It was from Dontae. He had texted Trent a picture of a hangman during their conversation. "You too old to be playing games."

"It's your funeral, but I got your back," Dontae joked. "Good luck tomorrow."

"I don't need luck. I make my money talking, and tomorrow will be no exception." Trent ended the call.

Despite his brave words, unease swirled through his insides. He questioned the sanity of revealing his truth and opening himself up for ridicule. Then he hunched his shoulders, remembering his father's advice when he had been teased as a youth. Laughter was just air. Wind. It would fade.

And build his bank account.

Chapter Four

November 11 had arrived with a dash of unexpected snow flurries followed by dark skies and rain. The weather matched the kind of day she had endured. Feeling the need to decompress, Selena had requested the cabdriver drop her off a couple of blocks away. Her boots crunched on a thin layer of ice and the wind whipped small ice particles into her neck.

While she walked, she reflected on her day. One of her clients, Theo Reinstall, hadn't showed up to his appointment nor answered her calls. Following her gut, Selena had notified the authorities. She had arrived at his place just in time to keep Theo from doing something rash. And permanent.

Selena knew firsthand how horrible it could be when family didn't accept your choices. Or support you. She'd offered Theo free additional services, which he had accepted. Theo had also caved and called his aunt and uncle. They had arrived, embracing him with so much love, Selena had dabbed at her eyes to keep from crying. When she'd left, Theo had been hopeful and in better spirits.

Sometimes, it was all about the ending despite the darkness at the beginning of the day.

Seeing that outcome gave Selena the strength to face her fear of baring her soul to thousands of faceless listeners tonight. Carla had hyped up tonight's broadcast, promising soul-baring stories from Selena and Trent.

She had taken the time to dress in a gray, knit, wraparound dress, gray tights and midcalf black boots, knowing her ensemble would be as much on display as her words tonight. She arrived at her destination and waved at the custodian who was pouring salt on the sidewalk. Selena opened the huge glass door and entered the station. She shook the flurries out of her hair and rushed upstairs to see Trent had gotten there ahead of her. As usual.

Today he wore a cream-colored hoodie that said Say Her Name, along with blue jeans and Timberland boots.

"Sorry I'm late," Selena said, noting the cameras and extra personnel milling about. "I had a crisis with a patient."

An assistant placed two bottles of water on the table before vacating the room.

Carla glanced at Selena's hair before her lips turned downward. "We won't have time to get your hair right." If her disapproval had a taste, it would be sour and tart.

Selena placed her coat on the rack and touched her ringlets. They hung like limp noodles against her cheekbones. "It's okay," she said in a reassuring tone. "People tune in to listen to me. Not see me." She dug into the purse and pulled out her lip gloss.

"I beg to disagree. Tonight, you're under a microscope and the camera lens will maximize every flaw," Carla said.

"What do you mean?"

"Thanks to Carla's serious publicity skills, we're going on camera tonight when we vomit the details of the most embarrassing time of our lives for our listeners' salacious pleasure," Trent supplied, splaying his hands. "In case you're wondering why we have more people crammed in here than usual."

Selena's brows raised. He sounded…snappy.

Carla cocked her head. "Really? This was both of your doing. I'm only here for the ride."

Trent shrugged. "Sorry. Poor attempt at humor."

Only that didn't sound like humor. Selena narrowed her eyes and scrutinized her cohost. He pulled on the neck of his hoodie and she could see the sweat lining his forehead.

"Whatever. We're going live in two minutes." Carla skittered out of the room.

"You're nervous," she observed.

"Yes. All day, my chest has been tight like I can't breathe." He placed a hand across his chest.

"Take deep breaths." She placed a hand on his arm. "Listen, it's not too late to back out if you don't feel comfortable."

He studied her for several seconds, rubbing his chin, then shook his head. "Nah. Nice try. I'm in. You're not hogging the spotlight all to yourself."

She gave a little laugh, refusing to admit the relief seeping through her bones. She didn't want to do this alone.

"And we're going live!" Carla bellowed from the booth.

Selena rushed to her seat, before the countdown. Trent greeted their listeners. "Welcome to another episode of *Weeknights with Trent and Selena...*" His deep bass voice washed over her, calming her nerves. Trent praised their listeners for giving them over a million views.

Soon it would be time for her to speak and Selena realized she hadn't practiced what she would say. She opened one of bottles of water and willed herself to relax. Just a small sip to wet her tongue because she didn't want her bladder full while she was on air. There was nothing more uncomfortable than trying to squeeze your legs tight and act normal when you had the urge to pee.

During the weather report, Selena scrounged for words. Then her eyes met Trent's. His warm ones communicated that he was with her. Her partner on air.

Selena gave him a small nod to signal her appreciation, squared her shoulders and leaned into the microphone, ignoring the heat of the lights from the camera on her face. Her brain scrambled while Trent took charge once again before turning over the air space into her hands.

Selena decided to wing it. Be brief. Matter-of-fact.

Licking her lips, she began. "I was thirteen years old when my father left my mother. I watched him walk out of her life and mine. That day was Valentine's Day. A day that was supposed to be one of love and hope was the day I became a prime witness to their final moments as a couple." She shifted in her chair, blocking out everyone around her and transporting herself back into the past. Ready to relive the horror of watching her parents' vicious argument and hateful words.

"I was there when my father ignored my mother's screams begging him not to leave her. Begging. I watched her crumple to the ground after he shouted, 'Get a life,' and stormed out of hers, out of mine, for good. I never saw him again. I remember rushing over to my mother, shaking and screaming her name. I cried for my father to come back until I was hoarse. Hours, until the neighbors banged on our wall for me to shut up. Shut up. Shut up." Pain like shards of glass whipped her heart. Selena paused to catch her breath and noticed those around her had tears in their eyes. She took a small sip for her dry throat.

"I can't imagine…" Trent said, giving her time to take another sip.

Then she continued, avoiding his eyes. Selena couldn't bear to see the pity in his. "I did. Shut up, that is. I have never mentioned my father by name again. But I wasn't the only person who got quiet that day." To her humiliation, her voice cracked. She placed a hand to her throat and whispered, "My mom did, too. But whereas I eventually found my voice and my calling, helping others, my mother never did. She was never the same." Selena cut off sharing more about her mother. A drop of water hit the table. She touched her face. Those were her tears. Selena gulped and used the back of her hand to brush her damp cheeks. "That's what Valentine's means to me." She sniffled. "So, yes, that's a day I can live without after what I saw happen to my mother and the day I lost my belief that love existed."

The lines were flashing. The phones were ringing.

But the occupants in the room were uncharacteristically silent.

The airwaves had stilled. Rare.

She dared to glance Trent's way and gasped. His face was wet, his lashes spiky, and his mouth was open, but no words came out. Selena averted her gaze and blinked to keep the tears from rolling down her face.

Carla saved the dead air by inserting two commercials.

Selena placed both hands on the table and stood. Then she dashed to the bathroom.

He'd had no idea.

No idea of the pain Selena hid under that practiced smile. Her composed demeanor was a shield hiding her past hurt. A hurt she had ripped open for the world to hear. It was… Raw. Real. Honest. Ripping at his guilt.

Trent gathered his index cards with his notes. He scanned the words on the lines he had planned to say.

Lies.

All lies.

Early that morning, Trent had composed a different tale designed to help him keep his macho image intact and engage his listeners.

But Selena…

Her bravery manifested his weakness brighter than the camera shining on his face. Trent tossed the cards in the bin under the table. Carla signaled they were going back on air. Selena slipped inside just before the count of one.

He reached across the table and clasped her hand. She squeezed his hand and whispered she was okay. He mouthed, *I'm not.*

Her eyes widened before she tightened her grip, mouthing, *You've got this.* After another commercial and an advertisement for their Thanksgiving mug and aprons, it was time for Trent to speak.

He grazed her knuckle with his thumb and commenced. "First, I want to applaud my cohost for sharing her story. Her dignity is unparalleled. Our inbox is flooded and I know many of you are eager to share. However, I, too, dread Valentine's Day more than you can imagine and I'm going to tell you why."

"We've been waiting for this all day. Right, ladies?" Selena said.

"Now, I admit feeling some anxiety," he said, knowing he was stalling. "But telling the truth takes courage and—"

"Get on with it," Selena interrupted. "By the time you get to the story, our time will be up. Unless that's your game plan."

Her teasing put him at ease. Trent cackled. "You're onto me."

From where he sat, he could see Carla jump with delight. She had her index finger pointing in the air. Their listeners must have doubled.

He grew serious. "A few years ago, I met a woman and I fell. Hard. I'll call her Rachel. Now, Rachel met all my checkboxes and I would have done anything for her. Including taking a vow of celibacy."

Selena's shocked gasp filled the room. She used her free hand to cover her mouth.

"Yes," he said with a nod. "For one year, we dated. I wined and dined her, took her on the best dates in some magical places, but I didn't *know* know her, if you get my drift. It wasn't easy, but I was a church boy and like Jacob waited for Rachel in the bible, I was willing to wait. On Valentine's Day, I went all-out. I flew her parents, my parents, my frat brothers and her best friends to Cancun, where I'd planned an elaborate surprise proposal."

"Wow," Selena said, eyeing him with newfound curiosity.

"I used tactics from every romantic movie—the rose petals, the band, the five-carat ring." He snorted. "Fellas, I went all the way old-school and asked her father's permission to marry her."

"So what happened?" Selena breathed, caught up in the tale. "Because I don't see a ring on his finger."

Trent rubbed his chin. "Turns out the joke was on me. Turns out, she hadn't been celibate. Instead, she had hooked up with one of my frat brothers. My best—er, former—best friend. I had brought him to Cancun on my dime. In an interesting turn of events, there was a proposal made, but it didn't come from me to her." His mortification sharpened his tone. "She left Mexico an engaged woman. To a different man."

"Dang," a voice said from behind.

Trent jerked his head around. The cameraman whispered, "Sorry. That's jacked up, man."

Selena spoke up. "Ladies, I'm sure we all know someone who didn't appreciate the love of a good man. If you do, why don't you call in and tell us about it. We're going to the phone lines after a few words from our sponsors."

Trent recognized her smooth diversion into another topic and thanked her for her thoughtfulness. Then they continued with the show. It was hours later before he would realize he was trending once again but for a different reason: #WhoIsRachel?

Chapter Five

Nine days after their revelations, Selena and Trent were still trending. Their listeners had skyrocketed, making the phone calls and emails overwhelming. Sponsors from all over were offering to help fund their singles ball thanks to Carla's efforts behind the scenes. Sitting in the cab on her way to the station, Selena scrolled through her social media accounts, dumbfounded by the sheer numbers. She had heard of TikTokers who gained 6.1 million followers overnight after posting a single video but Selena had no idea this would happen for her and Trent to this magnitude. It was both overwhelming and exciting. According to Carla, this was a good problem to have.

But beneath Selena's enthusiasm was worry.

Worry about how she would juggle everything she had to do.

She risked burnout but had kept her promise to Theo and had plugged in times to see him after the show. That meant she didn't get home until close to eleven most nights. Between her practice, her mother and the radio show, Selena felt pulled tighter than the cornrows the stylist had put in that morning before inserting the crocheted curls. Fearing heat damage from the camera, she had decided to give her natural hair a break. The midback-length ocean wave curls she now sported should last her a little over a month.

As a result of her hectic schedule, Selena had missed a regular visit with her mother. To make up for it, she was popping into the behavioral facility even though it was a Sunday. Generally, she used the weekends to recuperate, but her client demands had grown right along with her popularity.

Selena burrowed deeper into her coat and yawned before tipping the cabdriver. Her stomach grumbled its discontent at not being fed. She was out of coffee and hadn't had the time to visit the Whole Foods across the street. She would search her purse to see if she had anything to tide her over until lunchtime.

Pushing open the door to the Gracie Square Hospital, Selena entered the lobby and smiled. The soothing lights and soft music never failed to uplift her spirits. This is why she pushed. She checked in and then placed her purse into a secure locker, tucking the key in the pocket of her jeans. Then she made her way to her mother's private room, but Helen wasn't there. Selena frowned. It was a little after 11:30 a.m., and her mother would have already eaten breakfast. She decided to go up to the rooftop garden. Her mother found the foliage and green comforting.

A staff member waved. "She's with a group right now."

"Oh, I see." Selena ran a hand through her curls. "I forgot to check her schedule."

"It's quite okay. They will be done in ten minutes. Why don't you wait in the community room?"

With a nod, Selena went and sat in one of the couches behind a potted plant. She wished she could have carried in her cell phone and continued her game of solitaire. Within minutes, her mother arrived. Helen was with a couple other residents and had not spotted her.

Selena narrowed her eyes. Her mother was dressed in a striped shirt, color-coordinated jeggings and a pair of Crocs. Selena was pleased to see Helen had allowed them to comb her long hair into two neat braids. Her mother appeared to be talking and smiling.

Smiling.

Hurt punched her in the gut. She couldn't recall the last time she had seen her mother smile at her. Yet here she was smiling and laughing with others.

Selena shrank into the seat and watched as the staff placed them at a round table and took out playing cards. Helen's back was to her. Within minutes,

Helen and her friends were playing gin rummy. Now, it took some prodding, but Helen participated. At one point, her mother laughed at something said.

Laughed.

Furious tears sprang to Selena's eyes. All her mother ever had for her were spiteful words and sulking. Resentment flared and Selena jumped to her feet. She scurried over to her mom once the game ended.

"Look who's here to see you," the staff person said in a bright, encouraging tone.

Helen lifted her head. Her face dropped. Her body curved. She twisted away from where Selena stood. "Today's not Wednesday," she muttered.

"Should it matter what day your daughter comes to see you?" Selena fired back.

Helen shrugged. Then she picked up the deck of cards.

Selena tapped her mother's shoulder, her heart constricting when Helen stiffened. "Don't touch me. I heard your show. Talking our business for the whole world to hear."

"I didn't know you were listening." Selena's heart raced.

In a loud voice, her mother snapped out, "One of the nurses put it on even though I told her I didn't want to hear nothing from you. I don't even want to see you."

Knowing her face must have reddened, Selena closed her eyes to keep the tears from spilling. After an awkward pause, the staff member cajoled the other residents to go to another table. Selena slid into one of the vacant chairs.

"You don't have to speak to me like that, Mommy," she said in a furious whisper. "I don't deserve it."

"You more than deserve it. You look like your wicked daddy. I don't want to see your face. Get it through your thick head."

She gasped. "I pay for your care. I do my best to meet your needs because I love you. You know that, don't you?"

Helen pinned her with glacial eyes and a face filled with scorn. "So? You expect me to drop on my knees and praise you for doing your job?"

Stop arguing with her. It's futile. She's not well, Selena told herself even as the pain slaked through her heart, her mind and her soul. She curled her hands into fists and counted to ten. "Mommy, I came by to see you. To have a good visit with you. But if you are going to behave this way, I'll leave."

Helen cut her eyes. "Who cares? Tell you what. Don't come Thanksgiving. You hear me? Don't come. I'm better off without you."

Selena clutched her chest and backed away. "You don't mean that. You're my family…my only family."

"I mean it with every fiber of my being. Don't waste your time coming because I won't see you."

Trent walked into Sarabeth's ten minutes early on Monday morning, his legs sore from his workout. He had arranged to meet up with Selena at Sarabeth's at eight thirty so he was surprised to see Selena already seated at a table.

He pulled out a chair. Judging from the bags under her eyes, Trent surmised Selena hadn't slept well the previous night, but he knew better than to state that observation.

"You look smashing," he said with sarcasm, noting she had on a beige sweater dress, an ode to the fickle November seventy-degree weather boasting sunny skies.

She rolled her eyes, taking in his black sweats, T-shirt and light jacket. "You look sweaty…and not in a hunky, good way."

Holding up his arms to show his muscles, he waggled his brows. "I have to stay camera-ready. The ladies loved me showing my soft side on air."

"The men didn't agree," she said.

Neither did his boys, but Trent wasn't worried about all that. Showing his weakness made him strong. "Did you order?" he asked, picking up the menu.

"Yes. I got us both the Four Flowers smoothies, the avocado toast for me, plus the eggs and grains for you."

"Great choices." Trent said, putting down the menu and drumming his fingers on the table.

"I'm observant," she responded in a dry tone. Then she gave a little cough. "So tell me why we're meeting this early."

"Carla came up with preliminary plans for the singles ball. Did you see them?"

"No. I didn't get around to opening her email yet. What does it say?"

He leaned forward. "The network has given us a huge budget—carte blanche—for four hundred of our listeners. But we have to have a VIP section at a thousand dollars a seat."

Her mouth went wide. "What? Why? This is supposed to be our treat to our fans."

"A lot of celebrities—single celebrities—will want to attend," he said, wiping his mouth with a napkin. "But get this. The PR department wants to have a sixties' theme with some band I've never even heard of before. They suggest doing a giveaway, which includes a tour of Graceland. In two words, it sounds wiggity wack, and I can't cosign to that."

Selena threw her head back and laughed. "Did you really say 'wiggity wack' with a serious face?"

"Whatever. You know what I mean." He chuckled. "Their corny meter went up several notches on the scale. The producers really want us involved, so I think we've got to plan this ourselves."

Selena glanced at her watch. "I hear you and I agree high-level interception is needed. But I don't know if I will have the time."

He pinned her with a gaze. "For this, you must make the time." Their server came over with their meals and to collect the menus. They dug in. "This smoothie is so good. My taste buds thank you."

"I have a practice, Trent. The radio show isn't my only gig." Her brow creased with worry. "This time of year, things get tough for my clients. I can't abandon them."

"Maybe our show should be your only gig. I know this is none of my business, but it might be time you consider just doing one job."

"My friend, Nadine, said the same thing. She thinks I should quit the practice."

"Your friend is right." He cocked his head. "And let me remind you, the ball was your idea."

She groaned. "I was there. I remember." Selena closed her eyes, slurped her smoothie and then exhaled with satisfaction. "Hmm…my mouth is happy right now."

Goodness. That smile was sultry…seductive, and leading his mind into previously untraveled paths. What he wouldn't do to be that straw. But this was Selena. His cohost. Trent swallowed and redirected his gaze to the spinach on his plate. She took a bite of her avocado and moaned. Yes, moaned. Trent shifted. If she responded to food like this, how would she respond to— He shook his head. Not going there.

"When was the last time you ate?" he teased.

Her cheeks grew rosy, making her look…appetizing. "I'm sorry. My weekend ended on a sour note and food was the last thing on my mind." Her voice sounded velvety. Sexy, maybe.

Yeah…it had been a while and his body was reminding him of that fact. Pammie had been clingy since he'd told her his hours might change. Trent had stayed in over the weekend. Maybe he needed a midweek emergency hookup. "You need to eat," he said with much more concern than he should have.

"I know. I'll do better."

"I bet if I looked in your bag, I'd see chocolate candies or gummies. Those are not meals. Am I going to have to meet you for breakfast each morning to make sure you eat right?" He stuffed eggs in his mouth to give his mouth something else to do because it sounded too much like he was asking her out. Making a daily commitment. Trent couldn't do that.

She lowered her eyes and cupped her bag close, confirming his suspicions about the sweets inside. He gazed at her smooth skin and thought about how it would feel to the touch.

Forget midweek. He rubbed his chin. He needed lunchtime loving to take the edge off. Pronto.

"Are you okay?" she asked, her mouth covered with avocado. "You're looking at me funny."

"Am I?" he asked with a jolt. He reached over to brush the top of her head. "There was a fly on top of your head."

Her eyes went wide. "What? How embarrassing. Why didn't you tell me? How long has it been there?" She licked her lips. Twice.

His body jerked to life. He wasn't going to survive this meal if she kept that up.

"Must you ask so many questions?" he mumbled. "I was messing with you. I—I was thinking about this ball and a possible venue. Do you have any suggestions?" He focused on his food, keeping his eyes away from her face. Now he was eye level with her breasts.

That's it. He pulled up his phone and sent a text to Wonder Woman. The contact had earned that title. Then he looked up nearby hotels.

"Good idea," she said, probably thinking he was researching venues, and pulled out her phone. "While you're looking up some places, I'll read Carla's email."

Trent didn't correct her assumption. He leaned back into his seat when a response came back. It was a picture of her wedding ring with the words No longer in service. He sent a quick Congratulations, and deleted her from his phone. If he remembered right, Wonder Woman had wanted more than he could give. Besides, now that he thought about it, it would have been real grimy to use one woman to assuage the need for another.

Not that he *needed* Selena.

He could reach out to another contact but decided to actually look at some locations for their event. "If you have time today, we can check out some places."

"Let me check my calendar." She chewed on her bottom lip while she studied her phone. "I'm booked solid until eleven thirty, then I'm free until showtime," she said. "I can meet you for lunch and we can check out some places, if that works?"

"Yep. That works for me. I'll have one of our interns call ahead to schedule two or three places we can tour." He stood and dropped some bills on the table.

Reaching over, he tapped her on the nose. "It's a date. Don't be late."

Chapter Six

It's a date.

Carelessly tossed words that had snaked their way through her mind for the past two hours. Angled across the chaise longue in her office, Selena placed a hand on her forehead, hating the silence. Her clients—a mother and her teenage daughter—had canceled their session, giving her time to think. To dwell on Trent's words.

It's a date.

Her body tingled at the thought of meeting Trent for lunch. *Ugh.* Being in his presence this morning had brightened her monotone existence, like adding sprinkles to an ice cream cone. What she didn't get was why.

She stared at the ceiling fan looming above her. If her calculations were correct, it had been three years since she had been on an actual date. Prior to that, she had been in a relationship with an insurance agent whom she had met while on the way to a conference. Walter Thomas was more of a Netflix-and-chill, or rather, a let's-do-crosswords-and-chill or play-blackjack-and-chill kind of guy. She hadn't minded. Selena considered herself a cheap date. She was content going to a fast-food joint or taking a walk in the park. What she craved was companionship. What she didn't want was commitment.

Her safe boyfriend had shocked her with a proposal. She had looked into Walter's shiny, expectant eyes and envisioned a life filled with card games and playing Twister. Selena had ended things. Life with him would have been like a never-ending journey across a desert. Dull. Drab. Long. Not because she hated playing games or taking road trips. She'd just known she couldn't do it forever with Walter.

With a jolt, Selena realized she was lonely.

She frowned, tapped her chin and self-analyzed. Maybe her melancholia had nothing to do with the effect of Trent's words and everything to do with her mother. Normally, she would visit Helen when she felt like this, but Selena was the only person her mother didn't want to see. Deep down, she knew that, but Selena's inner child hoped that time would have healed her mother's personal wounds. However, time was a balm for those who sought it, for those who grabbed at its offer for a second chance. Maybe it was time Selena accepted what she couldn't change and stop wallowing in self-pity.

She swung her legs off the chaise and straightened. She couldn't change her mother. However, she could institute some minor changes and adjust her attitude. Like Nadine said, "Have some f-u-n." Selena lifted her chin. She didn't need anyone to have a good time. She could do fun all by herself. Selena chuckled at her corny sentiment.

She liked having a plan. Now all she had to do was execute.

The Valentine's Mingle for Singles was the perfect starting point to embracing her singleness. The dance didn't have to be just for her fans, it could be for her.

Her next appointment breezed into the room and plopped onto the couch, clutching her Gucci bag, and Selena directed her focus to her client.

While she worked, her enthusiasm grew. The next hour sped by. When Selena met Trent for lunch, her mood matched the beautiful day.

Trent strove to keep up with Selena on the busy New York City sidewalk. She had arrived at the diner and scarfed down her sandwich, before trading her pumps for sneakers. Then they had toured two of the venues with Selena spouting ideas for the dance. She was now moving at whirlwind speed, chattering on, as they made their way to Gotham Hall. Trent was too taken with watching her hand movements and her flashing eyes to focus on her words. He had never seen his cohost so animated.

It was sort of…cute.

"Let's wait until after Thanksgiving to book the talent," he suggested. "I was thinking we should find someone new who's also single. We could help launch their career."

For a second, her eyes dimmed, but then she gave a quick nod. "That makes sense, and I like the idea of helping a talented single or group of singles."

"What was that about?" he asked, putting a hand on her arm briefly and pinning her with a gaze.

"What do you mean?" she asked.

A man skirted around them as they blocked his path. The crowd meandered through them, and though a few recognized them, no one interrupted their conversation.

"You seemed to get a little sad when I mentioned Thanksgiving." He stepped into her personal space to allow a couple holding hands to pass without breaking contact. But he wasn't going to move until she answered him.

Selena toyed with the collar of her dress, her eyes darting here and there. He raised his brows. She flailed her arms. "Not everybody has a happy family. Let's just say Valentine's isn't the only holiday that can stir up some strong emotions." She resumed walking.

After a beat, so did he. He dared to extend an arm across her shoulders. "I don't know what's going on, but I'm here if you need to talk about it," he said, his tone gentle.

"I'm good. It's nothing I'm not used to." Selena gave a little laugh, her cheeks tinged with embarrassment. She touched his face. "But thanks. You're sweet."

"Don't tell nobody. I've a rep to maintain," he joked. But on the inside, he contemplated her words about being alone.

Trent rubbed his chin. As they entered the building, his main thought was that there was more to her cryptic words. He found he wanted to push, insist she tell him what was wrong, so he could fix it. That sentiment was new, outside the boundaries of their friendship. But his cohost was proud, independent, and wouldn't react well if he played hero. He knew enough about her from how she advised the women who called in that Selena favored mutual independence. Solving problems together. He lectured himself to let the matter rest. He had offered his assistance and she had declined. That should be it.

Only…it wasn't.

They entered the hall. Selena tilted her head and gasped. "Did you know this used to be a bank?" she whispered; her face enraptured.

"No. I had no idea." Trent said, awed by the majestic architectural design.

The click of heels captured his attention. A willowy blonde approached, looking regal, like royalty. She extended a hand and gave him a firm handshake.

"Welcome to Gotham Hall. I'm Antoinette, the personal event planner."

She then accepted Selena's outstretched hand. He bit his lip to keep from cracking up when Selena massaged her hand after Antoinette broke contact.

"What a grip," he said under his breath.

"I'm going to take you to the Grand Ballroom," Antoinette said.

They followed the blonde and stepped through brass doors and onto marble floors. As soon as he entered, Trent nodded. This was perfect. "We'll take it."

Selena gave him a shove. "We just got here." Her eyes widened and she placed her hands on her cheeks. "Look at that ceiling."

"That's a one-of-a-kind, stained-glass design. The walls are granite and the columns are limestone," Antoinette supplied.

"I'm surprised it's free on Valentine's Day," Trent observed.

"Surprising but true." Antoinette lowered her voice. "A couple canceled their wedding plans." She waved a hand. "Their fallout was a disaster. A soap opera come to life. I signed a NDA or I would tell you."

He could tell if he pressed, she would. But Trent understood the need for privacy, especially when you lived your life as a public figure.

"It's breathtaking." Selena beamed. "Their cancelation is our reservation." She wiggled with glee. "Everything is coming together."

Trent smiled at her excitement. He loved seeing this side to Selena. It was refreshing. Intriguing.

Antoinette laughed. "Great. Now that you've decided, let's get to the fun part. The food, the decorations."

"We'll also need a VIP area for our celebrity singles."

"The Oak Room would be perfect for that. I'll show you once we've finished with the paperwork."

They followed her into her office to make preliminary plans and to obtain a projected expense sheet.

Trent settled into the chair while the two women worked out the details, giggling like longtime friends. He interjected with suggestions, but was content to let Selena take the lead. He used that time to process her comment, which had stayed in the back of his mind. He could only arrive at one conclusion. And he could only offer one solution.

Before they parted ways, Trent took Selena's hands and asked, "Would you like to spend Thanksgiving with me?"

Chapter Seven

"Girl, what!" Nadine shrieked. "That is way past amazing."

Sitting in the back of the taxicab, Selena adjusted her AirPods and lowered the volume on her cell. Traffic had been at a standstill though the light had turned green. Thanksgiving was two days away and the holiday crowds were venturing in and out of the city. "I know. Carla called me with the news and it took everything in me to act normal. I wanted to jump on my bed like it was a trampoline."

Weeknights with Trent and Selena was now the top radio show in the nation. Number one. And the executives had their checkbooks ready. Selena had gotten three calls from other stations trying to poach her, offering her the chance to headline her own show with guaranteed syndication. But there was something to be said about loyalty. Though flattered, she would stay with Trent's show. Or rather, their show.

"I can't believe I'm best friends with the next Dr. Phil. Or Iyanla Vanzant."

She pursed her lips. "You're friends with me. Period."

"I hear you. You're a household name and you are finally getting paid what you're worth. Three hours a day, five days a week. Look at God. Won't He do it?"

"He can and He did. The best part is Trent and I got equal pay and shares starting now. Shares. I got to give him props. Trent did me right. I didn't have to wait until the new year. It starts now." She noticed the cabbie peering through the rearview mirror and lowered her voice. "I'm on my way to the studio to sign the contract before our show."

"Yes! I hope you bought a special pen. The best part about this whole thing is you get to occupy space with that fine specimen of manhood three feet away from you, every night."

"Well, it's not the best part. It's a part. The income. Helping others. Those are all better parts."

"Whatever. I don't know how you stand sharing his body heat all those nights and do nothing about it. If it were me…"

Selena chuckled. "I know. But I'm not you and, like I tell you—"

"You're all about you now," Nadine recited.

Selena voiced her new mantra every chance she could. "Self-love is important."

"Yeah. Yeah. A good man loving on me is even better. Whatever." Nadine squealed, "Anyhoo, we've got to celebrate later on tonight since I'm working tomorrow through Thanksgiving."

"That's crazy you have to work."

"Not everybody gets to spend the day with a man more delicious than the turkey, the mashed potatoes or gravy," she said.

Selena rolled her eyes. Ever since she had told Nadine about Trent's invite to Thanksgiving, her friend had ribbed her about it, advising Selena to wear her good underwear. "You could come with me," Selena had offered.

"I'll see if I can get somebody to cover my shift but the holidays are our busiest times. The turkey fryers mean fires, burns, injury. You name it. We see it. Sad but true. I don't mind because that's the life of an ER nurse and they pay me overtime, so it's all good. So, when I work, I work hard. And when I play, I play even harder."

"All right, let me know." Selena disconnected the call just as the cabbie arrived. *TRENT'S*

Seeing Trent pace the edge of the curb, Selena's heart skipped a beat, knowing he had been waiting for her. When the driver pulled up, he rushed toward the cab to open the door. He wore black slacks and a white dress shirt with the top buttons undone for the occasion. With his shape-up, he had definitely earned a second or third glance.

As soon as she exited, she jumped into his arms. "We did it.".

"Yep. Carla came through. Big-time."

They rocked with excitement. The scent of cedar... sandalwood wafted through her nostrils and she inhaled. Selena admitted to herself that she enjoyed the feel of his powerful arms about her. To her recollection, this was the first they had hugged a hug that never ended. Usually, they fist-bumped. That's what they had done when she had accepted his invitation to Thanksgiving dinner. It had been...thoughtful and sweet.

With a regret she would never admit, Selena ended their embrace. Together they walked to the entrance and she thanked him for holding her door open. Selena wrapped her arms about her when she passed, feeling a weird sense of awareness. Shy almost to look him in the eyes. Then she gave herself an internal shake. This was Trent, her buddy. She blamed this heightened cognizance on Nadine. Her friend's comments were putting ideas in her head that didn't need to be there.

They went into the elevator, both quiet. She wondered what he was thinking and stole a glance at him from under her lashes. Seeing he was focused on something on his phone, Selena released a deep breath.

"I'm nervous," she confessed as the elevator went past their floor.

"Don't be." He placed a hand on her shoulder. She tensed. The contact burned through her blazer. She felt everything. From his palm to the tip of his fingers. He shifted, bringing those long fingers closer to her cheek.

Selena didn't know what was happening, but this needed to stop. Trent wasn't the kind of man she needed in her life. Except for business. He was too... laid back. Too...smooth. She inched her way to the corner of the car, pretending to read the sign posted.

They continued in companionable silence until they entered the boardroom. Trent pulled out one of the leather chairs around the long oval table for her and then took the seat beside her. Carla sat across them, her face beaming brighter than a hot Jamaican sun. Three men and a woman sat at the opposite end. There were three folders bearing hers and Trent's names as well as Carla's.

"Before we begin," Trent said, "Since we're looking at three hours, I wanted to ask if you would consider moving our show time up to 4:00 p.m.?"

Selena frowned. Her sessions sometimes ran close to 5:00 p.m. Trent should have discussed this with her first before broaching the subject here.

One of the men nodded. "That would be a great idea. That time frame would coincide with our vision for the show's expansion. We're looking to do the radio version of *Good Morning America*."

Carla chimed in. "I'd love to hear your thoughts."

Selena used that opportunity to give Trent a light jab in the arm, widening her eyes once he made contact. "I have a practice, or did you forget?"

"I have a—" He stopped and then patted her hand. "I'm sorry. You're right. I should've discussed it with you first. It's just I have a…special commitment."

She smirked. Special commitment? He must mean his late nights with his lady friends. "A heads-up would've been nice."

"Selena?"

She heard her name being called and cocked her head. "I apologize. I missed the question." Great, a therapist who didn't listen. Not a good look.

"How do you feel about the earlier hours?" the CEO asked. Josephine Hughes was of Jamaican and Chinese descent but her accent was barely discernible. The fact that she was fair, with waist-length hair she kept in a bun and blue-gray eyes, made many curious about her race and doubt her tenacity. That was how she'd become the head of the network under the age of thirty, earning her, as Jamaicans would say, "Much respect."

Selena tapped the table with her fingers. It would work if she closed her practice. She leaned back into her chair as that thought took hold like a wraparound vine. She wet her lips with her tongue. "Can you give me a month?"

She needed to find proper replacements for her clients. Particularly Theo. Or…she could hire freelance therapists… Just thinking about this huge shift made her pulse accelerate. Instantly, her mind churned, questioning whether she was doing the right thing. At the same time, she acknowledged, her sheer exhaustion at the end of the day from doing too much.

"Of course. We would launch early January," she said. "We have to strike now, while you two are hot commodities. After both your on-air confessions, we are struggling to keep up with our listeners' demands. They want more of you two, and we want to grant their wishes."

Selena released a plume of air. As they spoke around her, her heart bemoaned the fact that her beloved practice would close. She had helped so many people. That place had been a haven for many hurting souls. She swallowed and blinked back the tears threatening to spill.

Carla's eyes shone. "Every night we end the show with listeners pleading for one more call. Since this started with Valentine's Day, how about we schedule the launch then? We could debut the expanded show at that time."

"That's a great idea but I would prefer sooner rather than later," Trent said.

Once Trent voiced his opinion, the other men nodded. "Agree."

"January second," Josephine said. Her voice held authority. No one argued. Everyone—Selena included—agreed.

The elevator ride to their floor was silent. Selena stood with her bag tucked under arm, her eyes pinned at the metallic doors. Trent leaned against the back wall, staring at her.

"So you just gonna stand there and not talk to me?"

"Isn't this how you like it?" she asked, her lip poked out. "A silent partner?"

"Silence doesn't look good on you," he said, giving her arm a playful bop. "I had a good reason to ask for those hours but I should have discussed it with you first." He needed to be home with Pammie. His sister had begun texting him whenever he was late. Trent had given her a cell phone a few months ago. Pammie used it to watch her TV shows on YouTube, play her music, and take pictures. She had finally mastered texting using Siri.

Selena faced him. "This is our show now, Trent. You're not the BMOC calling all the shots just to please your ladies." She snarled the last word.

Trent wanted to correct her assumption that he was womanizing on a weeknight, but he simply shrugged.

The elevator paused and the doors swished open. In a flash, she was out the door and heading toward her dressing room.

"I'm not trying to be the big man on campus," he said, catching up. Trent reached out and held her arm. She bristled beneath his touch. "I'm sorry. It won't happen again."

Her shoulders relaxed and she gave a tentative smile. "Thank you. Apology accepted. Now let me go get my hair and makeup done."

"Yes, go," he teased, "you've got all this fineness to compete with."

She chuckled before scuttling to her dressing room.

Trent exhaled, glad he and his cohost were no longer at odds. He couldn't let anything off-air interfere with their rapport on-air. Whistling, he headed into his oversized room to change into his jeans and sweater before the show began.

This sweater featured a picture of Tamir Rice, a twelve-year-old black boy who was shot and killed on November 22, 2014 by a policeman for yielding a toy gun. Trent's heart squeezed when he imagined the young man immortalized at that age forever, making history for the wrong reason, just like Emmett Till. He shook off his grief, wishing he could be a bigger voice for injustice. Like Colin Kaepernick and others, Trent fought with silent persistence. As long as the producers allowed it, he would wear the shirts. They promoted many insightful discussions online. They kept the senseless deaths of these individuals in people's hearts and minds.

Trent strode into the booth feeling heavy-hearted and greeted the cameramen with a head nod. When Selena arrived, he went over the itinerary before deciding to lighten the mood. "Let's start with the announcement for the Valentine's Ball instead of waiting until the end of the show. Mess with Carla a bit. What do you think?"

"Carla will have a fit if you deviate from our script, but I say go for it." Her eyes held mischief.

They fist-bumped.

Carla gave the signal from the booth.

He waited for the usual countdown then began. "Welcome, welcome, to another night with Trent and Selena. Before we get started, Selena and I wanted to make a special announcement."

From his peripheral view, he could see Carla waving a hand to get his attention, but pressed on. "You have been emailing and calling about Valentine's Day and we want to celebrate you. With the help of our generous sponsors, we are throwing a party. The party of all parties. That's right, ladies and gentlemen, guys and gals, four hundred of our lucky callers will be provided free tickets to our first ever Valentine's Mingle for Singles Ball at Gotham Hall in Midtown."

The phone lines started flashing.

Selena chimed in. "Twenty of you will get access to our special VIP room where you will mingle with some of our A-listers. Celebrity friends, that's you. Have your people reach out to our people to purchase tickets."

"If you want in, write the show, tell us why," Trent said before transferring to the weather forecaster.

As soon as they went to commercial, Carla came storming in. "You did this on purpose," she fumed. "You were supposed to talk about Thanksgiving memories first. I had a whole big to-do planned, promos, banners, to reveal the ball and you just…" She raked a hand through her hair. "Now everything's all messed up."

Trent and Selena made eye contact before bursting into laughter.

"You two are like children," Carla snapped before stomping out of the room.

A scent of vanilla hit his nostrils. Trent studied his cohost's side profile. She had her head tilted back, revealing a long, graceful neck as she laughed at their antics. He loved the throaty, velvety sound. "No, everything is just right."

Chapter Eight

This can't be right. Selena approached the address on Lafayette Street that Trent had texted her with narrowed eyes. She shook her head and reviewed the address again, wiping her brow, feeling the effects of the vicious afternoon sun. *This can't be where he lives.* A huge sign displayed Community Hearts.

"Don't tell me this man played me." She frowned, squeezing her toes in her new Manolo Blahniks, sorry she hadn't made the cabdriver wait. She ran her tongue over her teeth and contemplated. Trent wouldn't be that cruel. He wouldn't have invited her to dinner as a gag. Not on Thanksgiving. She just knew this man hadn't sent her to a shelter on Thanksgiving.

She perched the box of frozen Italian bread-

sticks—her Thanksgiving dinner contribution—
between her knees and pulled out her phone.

I'm here. I think... she texted him. Not sure this address is correct???

It is. LOL. I'm coming.

Selena shoved the box of breadsticks in her tote,
exhaled and tapped her feet, feeling kind of stupid.
He had told her to dress casual but, of course, she
hadn't. Selena figured Trent lived in a ritzy penthouse. There was no way she was going to arrive at
his place for the first time and not show out. So she
had chosen a pair of cream slacks and a sweater—
business casual. She did have the sense to pack sen-
sible flats and, boy, was she glad she had.

The door opened and Trent stepped outside wearing his usual jeans and a sweater with what looked
like a crazy-looking pumpkin in the center. Yes, a
pumpkin. "Hey! You made it," he said then glanced
at his watch. "Right at 3:00 p.m."

She inched forward. "I run a practice. I do know
how to be on time." Especially since she had dressed
two hours in advance.

He smirked. "Come on inside."

She walked through the huge metal door and
froze. It was a shelter. A shelter with some great
gospel music and heavenly smells. The scent of cin-
namon floated from across the room. She'd bet on

that being candied yams. Her eyes scanned the large space filled with long rectangular tables. There had to be about two hundred people here. The line for the food table was lengthy.

"I told you to wear sneakers," Trent said, eyeing her shoes.

"I… I have my flats." She placed a hand on her hip. "What's going on?"

He patted Selena on the back and shooed her further into the room, toward the direction of the food line. "Family tradition. My parents made a point of serving Thanksgiving meals to the homeless. Every year, they would bring my sister and I to help. Said it would keep us grateful. Now that I'm older, I continue this, funding it in their honor."

She watched his confident stride and said, "Sister?" She searched her memory. To her knowledge, she had never heard Trent mention he had a sibling.

He nodded. "Yes. Do I have to tell you how I got one of those?"

"Quit being silly," she said, cracking up. "I didn't know you had one. You never talk about her."

"Pammie's…special" were his cryptic words before he beckoned her to follow him. He greeted a few people on the way, appearing at ease, taking the time to ask about this one or that one before entering the kitchen.

"I'll get you an apron," he said, helping her out of her light jacket and hanging it on the chair.

"Oh, we're not eating?" she asked. Glad that she had chosen a dark top with her clothes.

"Not yet. This is about helping people less fortunate. You'll be with me. We're serving pies and ice cream, so grab a couple disposable gloves." He pointed to a box on the counter.

She lowered her gaze. "Sorry. I didn't mean..." She must sound selfish and uncaring. Entitled. In her defense, she hadn't eaten all day. Still, like Trent said, this wasn't about her.

"No worries. I should've explained," he said.

"Yes, you should have." Her voice held an edge. "I would have gladly helped. And dressed accordingly."

"I'm sorry. I was going for the element of surprise."

He shifted. "I can see now that this wasn't the right approach." Stuffing a hand in his jeans pocket, he asked, "Does this mean you're leaving?"

Selena shook her head. "Of course not, but I would have snacked or something if I knew. Where do I get started?"

Trent pointed to her feet. "I'll show you what to do. Let me get you an apron while you get out of those fancy heels."

Selena changed her shoes and placed the apron over her head, thankful she hadn't followed her inclination to straighten her curls. It was hot in here. The outside temperature was close to sixty degrees today and the day before had been in the thirties. The shelter hadn't adjusted the thermometer. Heat wafted through the vents and sweat already lined her forehead.

Clasping her hands, Selena trailed behind Trent, sliding her gaze over the turkey, mashed potatoes, candied yams, corn and green beans. Her stomach grumbled but the people here may not have eaten a proper meal for days. She could wait. Putting on her gloves, Selena stood with Trent and served the community.

She noted there were singles, old, young, families. People of all races and sizes. None of those disparities mattered. They were all there to have a basic human need met. And to chat it up with Trent. There was a lot of joy and goodwill, despite their circumstances. After watching a family hugging and laughing together, awareness hit her heart.

These people might be poor by society standards, but they were richer than she was where it mattered most. Love.

After working for close to two hours, a couple of volunteers came up to say they would be relieving them, then left to get aprons and disposable gloves. Trent said they would keep the kitchen open until 7:00 p.m. that night.

She looked at him and leaned in. "Thank you for inviting me."

Selena disposed of her gloves and wiped her hands on her apron before washing and drying them. She had to have served about two hundred people slices of an assortment of pumpkin, apple and cherry pie. Trent had scooped the vanilla ice cream from industrial-sized containers. His sense of humor had kept Selena and the people entertained.

"It's eye-opening, isn't it?" he asked, giving her a nudge.

"Yes. I can't think of a better way to spend the day."

He gave her a tender look. "Neither can I."

She slid her gaze away.

A young woman half skipped, half walked as she approached. Selena had noticed her playing with some children earlier. She had on a designer tracksuit, Michael Kors glasses and soon-to-be-released sneakers. Her hair had been done in shoulder-length knotless braids.

"Hey, Pammie," Trent said, greeting the young woman. "Did you eat?"

This was Pammie? Selena blinked to keep from giving Trent a look of surprise. He was right. Pammie was special. But Selena hadn't known his words meant his little sister was an individual with special needs. He must have kept her out of the spotlight, because Selena had been with him for years and hadn't known.

"Yes. Ms. Mindy fed me," Pammie said, moving her hips to the music. "But she said I must come to you. She had to go home."

Trent nodded. "Okay, sweetheart. Thanks for letting me know." After he introduced her, he jutted his chin to a chair a few feet away and addressed Pammie. "Why don't you wait there for me? I'm going to get myself and Ms. Selena something to eat."

Selena had sampled a small piece of pie but her stomach was ready for some of that Thanksgiving dinner. She had thought about taking a bite of one of the frozen breadsticks, which she would toss before leaving, that was still in her tote. That's how hungry she was. But she felt a sense of fulfillment, of purpose.

Pammie pointed to the pies. "May I have a piece?"

"Not too much," Trent said in a gentle tone. He then addressed Selena. "I'll go get our food. Can you keep an eye on her?"

Selena nodded and served his sister a small slice. Pammie gave her a bright smile, her face beaming. Selena's heart pounded. She didn't have much interaction with children or people with disabilities. But she was a therapist and skilled at conversation so she should be able to keep Pammie entertained. However, she needn't have worried. While she ate, Pammie supplied a steady stream of information about her favorite rapper. Selena found the young woman engaging. She nodded and asked questions, though she had no idea who Pammie was talking about. When Pammie was finished, Selena helped her wipe her mouth and showed her where to toss her plate.

Trent returned, holding two half-open Styrofoam containers. She appreciated the steam coming from under the lid and the yummy smells.

"I was worried they would run out of food."

"That's never a concern," he said, sitting across from her and next to his sister. He placed one of the containers in front of Selena along with individually wrapped utensils. "We usually have enough for everyone to take home a box or two."

"Wow." Her mouth hung open. "That's a lot of leftover food."

"There're a lot of hungry people." He tore open the plastic and retrieved a fork.

His words sank in. Selena tilted her head and observed him from under her lashes. Trent Moon was a generous, caring man. His actions made her aware of how little she did beyond her personal circle. She made a vow to change that.

Pammie rested her head on his shoulder. "Can I go play with those kids?" she asked, pointing to a group of girls holding dolls and Hula-Hoops.

Trent rubbed his chin and looked to where she pointed. "Yes, that's fine. I know them. But we're leaving soon." With a nod, she scampered off.

"You're good with her," Selena said after saying grace. She dug into the mashed potatoes. They were creamy and delicious.

"Thank you. I had to learn. When my parents passed, I applied for custody." He stuck some of the green beans in his mouth. "As a celebrity, I did everything I could to keep her out of the spotlight and from scrutiny. But now that she's older, I finally caved and allowed her to have a TikTok account to showcase her singing. She has an amazing voice and has been preparing for her big launch."

She heard the pride in his voice. "You sound like her biggest fan."

"That's because I am." He beamed.

She liked the man she was getting to know beneath the affable exterior. Selena tilted her head. "You're nothing like I thought you would be. You know that?"

Selena had been a trooper. Trent had registered the shock on her face when she had arrived at the shelter and had expected Selena to make an excuse or leave early, especially dressed in her fine clothes. Instead, she had helped him feed those in need with exuberance, ignoring the stain on her cashmere sweater. Selena had worked next to him, standing on her feet for hours, without a single complaint.

But it was her interaction with Pammie that warmed Trent's heart, that made Trent invite Selena to his place and partake with another family celebration. That, and he wasn't ready to tell her goodbye, though he wouldn't dwell on the why.

Trent settled into the seat of the cab as they journeyed across town to his high-rise apartment near Central Park. He closed his eyes and half listened while Pammie chatted about her unicorn collection, clutching Selena's hand. Pammie was enamored with Selena, having told her she loved her at least three times during the course of the ride.

Trent had mouthed an apology above his sister's head, but Selena had waved a hand. "It's quite okay."

When the cab arrived at the Upper East Side's Carhart Mansion, Pammie had declared Selena her new best friend. They greeted the doorman holding open the carved wood door and went up the short flight of stairs into the lobby and to the elevator. Trent heard Selena's sharp intake of breath as she admired the opulence of the place in which he lived.

The elevator opened to a reception hall of his five-bedroom, four-and-a-half bath, bi-level home. Trent told Selena to close her mouth and took her on a tour, with Pammie trailing behind. Selena oohed and aahed at the living room boasting twelve-foot ceilings, a wood-burning fireplace and a kitchen with custom countertops, SubZero and Viking appliances. Her eyes bulged at the library, rec room, his office and the terraces that provided a majestic view. He skipped the bedrooms, except for Pammie's, before they returned to the family area.

"This is… This is spectacular," Selena breathed, splaying her hands. "I can't even find the words."

Trent smiled. "The first time I saw this place, I held my stomach, battling the urge to run. It was too much for me." He shrugged. "But, eventually, this seven-thousand-plus square feet of space became home." He pointed to the pictures of his family, mostly of Pammie. "When my parents died, I remember vividly how we had to leave the place we had lived in for all our lives and that added to my devastation. That's why I purchased this as soon as I could. The son of the previous owner was eager to sell and he gave me a great offer. Because I made some good investments, I now own it outright. No one's going to tell me I have to leave if I don't want to, and Pammie will always have security." He gestured for Selena to take a seat.

"I get that," Selena said, settling into the couch. Pammie was right next to her, cuddled under her arm and playing with her curls. "After my dad left, my home life was shattered. I couldn't wait to leave. I've felt like a nomad ever since."

Her voice held a sadness that tugged at Trent's heart. He wanted to ask more but decided not to push. Like him, Selena was private. She would tell in her time.

He cleared his throat. "So, to continue the Moon family tradition, I am going to make popcorn and we will watch *Halloween*."

"I like that movie," Pammie said, giving Selena a look of adoration.

Trent's heart constricted. He appreciated Selena's patience with Pammie. He could see that his sister craved female companionship and felt a pang knowing he could never meet that need. Pammie had started asking him if he was going to get a wife. Trent always diverted the topic but maybe…things would change.

"When I was your age, I was still scared of that

film," Selena said, giving Pammie a tender look. "You're brave."

"I think it's funny," Pammie said, picking up the remote to turn on the Apple TV.

Trent laughed. "This is her second year watching with me. She falls asleep halfway through."

"I'm going to stay up this time." Pammie bounced.

Hiding his smile, Trent stood. "I'm going to make the popcorn."

"I would help you but I'd burn it," Selena said.

"No worries. I got this." He went into the pantry to get the kernels and then set up the popcorn maker. Adding salt, butter and herbs, Trent made a fresh batch, filling three large bags then joined Selena and Pammie who were watching something on YouTube. They dug into the snack.

"This is good," Selena said, holding some in her hand.

"There's nothing like freshly popped kernels. Don't stuff your mouth," Trent said to Pammie.

"Come sit next to me," Pammie said to him.

Trent complied and put on the movie. Within minutes, they became engrossed in the film. He cracked up at Selena's shrieks. The fear in her eyes was real. Sure enough, Pammie stretched out and fell asleep, resting her head on Selena's lap and her legs on his. In that instant, though they were in a large area, the air circled around them like an invisible cord and tightened. He felt a strong sense of family. Looking at Pammie and Selena, he swallowed his natural instinct to protest and let the feeling fill his being. Now he felt fear, but for a different reason. It felt right. It felt right being here with Pammie and Selena. Fulfillment. He stopped there, not ready to explore what that meant. Instead, he turned on the surround sound and increased the volume on the TV, hoping to drown out the pleas of his heart.

Chapter Nine

Selena looked at the six-hundred-and-forty-nine-dollar price tag on the one-shoulder, embellished minidress and cringed. Not at the price. But at the color. At the length.

She stood in the dressing room of the trendy Soho designer gown boutique in her nude underwear and addressed Nadine, who waited outside the door. "I don't know about this. Where is the rest of the dress?"

"Girl, please. Try it on," Nadine begged.

"I'm sorry I let you talk me into going dress shopping."

It was the Monday afternoon following Thanksgiving weekend, two days until the last day of November. Selena had invited Nadine to go to the club

with her and Trent since her friend was off Saturday night. Nadine had agreed, especially when she'd
heard they would have VIP access. But Nadine had
insisted Selena not attend in her business attire and
talked Selena into trying on a tangerine-colored
dress with a pair of gold heels. Selena shied away
from heels because of her height, but she'd agreed
to put them on to appease her friend.

Nadine pounded on the door. "Don't make me
come in there. You've spent most of your adult life
in the books, taking care of your mom or on the job.
You're barely out of your thirties, you can let your
hair down and have some fun."

Those last three words reminded Selena of her
promise to herself. Have some f-u-n. After the morning she had spent breaking the news to her clients of
her practice closing near the end of the month, she
needed to have fun. Some of her patients had cried,
pleaded with her not to close. Others had wished her
well despite the pain in their voices.

The toughest call by far had been the one she'd
made to Theo. But he had eased her mind when he
shared he was relocating and asked for her assistance
with recommending a therapist. Selena had known
just the person—Myron Goodson—and he had open-
ings. Theo would be in good hands.

"Selena?" she heard again.

"All right. All right. Give me a minute." Selena
drew in a deep breath, slipped the dress over her
head and stepped into the heels. It fit like skin on a

snake. She curved her body and looked into the mirror. Her butt was saying *Hello*. Her eyes went wide. Her "girls" were saying an even bigger *Hello*. "I don't know about this," she mumbled and opened the door.

Nadine's eyes popped. She gestured for Selena to spin around. "Wow. You look like an Amazon goddess and, girl, you are working those heels." Hanging the red, teal, and black dresses she held on the hook, she said, "I can't wait to see you in these."

Selena yanked on the hem of her dress. "It's too short." Great. Now her boobs were exposed.

"Nah, girl. That dress is perfect. It's hugging your bodankadonk like it never wants to let go." Her friend gyrated. "The men are going to be lapping after you like dogs hungry for a treat." She gave a howl. An actual howl.

"Girl, stop acting like you have no sense." Selena laughed. "I'm not going man-hunting. This is a work night for me. And the men will be too enamored with you to glance my way."

Nadine grabbed her arm. "Don't chicken out on me. You're getting this dress. It brings out your skin tones." Then she sat on the small bench in the room, crossed her legs and folded her arms. "Try on the others."

She tried on the teal dress next. "I don't even look like me," she whispered, wondering what Trent would think of her new look. "I look like a video vixen."

"Yes, you do," Nadine said with admiration.

"I didn't mean that as a compliment. I want to be

taken seriously. Seen as a professional." She ran her hands down her body. "Not seen as a sex symbol."

"Why can't you be both?" Nadine cocked her head. "You're sexy and smart. Own it. You don't have to be one or the other. That archaic belief is over and done with. It's time for you to get with the times. And like I said, you're going to a c-l-u-b. Nobody wants to see grandma getting down on the dance floor. And you know Trent is going to be dressed to the nines. You can't let him outdo you."

"I'm not in competition with Trent. For me, it's very much about finding talent for our ball. I have no plans of dancing. And I don't look like anybody's grandma," Selena said, hurt at her friend's description and at the possibility of Trent seeing her that way.

"Okay, that was a low blow. I was just trying to make a point, and you know I don't mean it." She was right. Selena knew her friend meant well. Nadine jumped to her feet. She reached behind Selena's head, unwrapped the scrunchie and freed her mane from the bun.

"What are you doing?" Selena asked, chewing on her bottom lip.

"You'll see." Raking her fingers through Selena's hair, Nadine framed the curls about Selena's face. Then she turned her toward the mirror.

Selena gasped. She leaned forward a bit, gaping at the siren staring back at her.

"You look beautiful," she said. "That's what I see. Embrace you. All of you."

Selena nodded. "Thank you, friend." She thought of Trent seeing her like this and excitement shivered through her insides. "I'll try on the black one next. Why don't you find me some shoes for these?"

"I sure will."

After another hour of shopping, the women decided to have pizza, hot wings and celery sticks for dinner. Selena had skipped lunch, so she wasn't concerned about counting calories.

"This is so worth the extra hour on the treadmill," Nadine said, biting into her slice.

Selena patted her stomach. "These wings are giving me life right now. They are sooooo good." The breaded wings had been fried extra-crispy before they'd added the buffalo sauce. It was only because she feared her photo featured in a "Celebrities Are Like Us" section of a magazine, that she wasn't licking her fingers. Instead, she cleaned her fingers on one of the wet wipes they provided.

"Have you spoken to your mom?" Nadine asked, already on her second slice.

"I called and the staff told me she was having a bad day. So I didn't bother asking to speak to her. My psyche couldn't handle her rejection the same day I said goodbye to my clients."

"Good decision." She sipped her water before reaching for a wing. "Were you able to provide them with referrals?"

Selena nodded. "Yes, to those who wanted one." She had spent all weekend working on a list of potential therapists to recommend to clients during their final sessions. She bit into her slice of pizza. "I feel guilty though, Like I'm abandoning them."

"They will be all right. You've been running non-stop like a hamster. On a wheel. In a cage. Closing the practice was the right decision. Soon, you'll be earning close to seven figures and in a position to employ others to do what you can't. Start a foundation or fund mental health programs."

Selena snapped her fingers. "That's a good idea."

"Yeah, I'm a pro at spending money. Your Amex card can testify. I would be a master at being rich if the good Lord saw fit to do so." Nadine snickered.

"Do you think you would want to run a foundation if I started one? It would be a chance to use your experience and your administration expertise in a much less stressful environment."

Nadine's eyes watered. "You would trust me to do that?"

"Of course. Shame on you for even asking that question." She reached for another wing. "I'll talk to Trent about this. He has a couple foundations. I'm sure he would give me the right pointers to get started. In fact…" She pulled up her messages on her cell phone. "Let me text him now and ask so I don't forget."

"Wow. You're for real. In that case, I'd be honored," Nadine said, sniffling and wiping her face.

"Not as honored as I am to have you for a friend."

"With friends like you, who needs enemies?" Trent joked. He stood behind the counter of his kitchen, working the homemade pizza dough. His first job had been at Pizza Hut and he was especially good at thin crust. He had installed a coal-fired grill on one of the three terraces on his property.

"You can't expect us to take your side over this gorgeous woman's," James teased.

Both he and Dontae had stopped in for his weekly Sundaes on Hump Day with Pammie, to celebrate Pammie's TikTok debut and then catch a game on his theater-sized television. It didn't matter the game, as long as there was something playing, they would be watching.

Trent gave an exaggerated sigh and slumped his shoulders. "Fine, you win. We'll do sundaes after pizza." He had suggested they make pizzas and ditch their weekly sundaes, but had known Pammie wouldn't go for that. Just like he knew his friends would take her side. Pammie had them all wrapped around her hand, and she knew it. Right now, the three of them were watching *Tangled*, each holding a unicorn.

"Yay!" Pammie squealed, rocking her hips from side to side. "I told you that would be a good idea."

Trent hoped she felt that way once the cheese and ice cream hit her stomach. Like him, she was lactose intolerant. He was glad he had more than enough bathrooms for everyone. A thought came to him. He then opened up the cabinet where he kept his vitamins and medicines. It was high enough so Pammie couldn't get to them. He rummaged until he found their lactose pills. Taking one, he called Pammie over to take one, as well, breaking it in two.

"You guys need a lactose pill?" he called out.

"Nah. That's for punks," James said, patting his rock-hard abs.

"I'm good."

Trent chuckled. "All right, tough guys." He added his special pizza sauce and a generous amount of mozzarella cheese. After placing it in the wood-fired pizza oven, Trent worked on two more large pies. A couple slices wouldn't be enough for his friends.

"Ooh. Is Ms. Selena coming?" Pammie asked, clapping her hands.

Every day she asked for Selena. Trent noticed both James and Trent waited for his answer. "No, sweetheart. It's just us and Uncle James and Uncle Dontae, like always."

Her shoulders drooped. "Okay."

Trent slapped his forehead. Talking about Selena jarred his memory. He'd promised to send her the information on starting a foundation. He used his cell phone to retrieve his files through Dropbox and sent her a share link and a quick text. *We'll talk later.*

James came over to join him. "Is that Selena you're texting?"

"Yeah. I forgot I needed to send her some info."

"How are things going with that dance you're planning?"

He gestured for James to pour the sauce on one of the pizza doughs. "It's coming along. We found the venue. Now all we have to do is find the talent. Selena and I are meeting up at the club this Saturday night."

"Oh, are you coming to the Lounge? I'm working that night. Maybe I can meet her. Is she seeing someone?"

Trent felt a twinge and his stomach muscles tightened. "Yes, we'll be there, and I don't know anything about Selena's romantic life." He didn't like the idea of James scoping out Selena but he hated sounding bothered about it.

"Whoa?" James jabbed his arm. "Are you hitting that? Cuz you sound all possessive, like it's a problem that I'm asking about her."

"No," he huffed, "I'm not. Hitting that. Don't be all crass about it. If I come across like I'm coming at you, I apologize." He sprinkled a generous amount of cheese on the dough. "I'm not possessive, just protective. She's one of the good ones. You know what I'm saying?"

"I hear you," James said, giving him the side-eye.

Trent went outside to retrieve the first pizza and to put the others in the oven. Why was he on edge because James had asked about Selena? It wasn't like James wasn't good people. Trent had no reason to block his intentions—except for the fact that he wanted her for himself. That truth made his stomach knot. He shook off the revelation. Nope. He wasn't going there. Selena wasn't the hit-it-and-quit-it type. She needed something lasting.

He heard footsteps and turned to see Pammie behind him. "Be careful. This pizza is hot."

Pammie wrung her hands. "Are you going to let me spend the night at Emily's?" she asked.

"I told you I would think about it," Trent said. He already knew the answer. He just didn't want to tell his sister no.

"Yes, but that was a long time ago."

"It's only been hours, Pammie."

Her lips quivered and she stomped her feet. "I want to go. I'm a big girl. I can go to a sleepover if I want to."

Dontae came outside. "Do you need help?" he asked, which was code for, I'm hungry and ready to eat. He looked between them and must have sensed the tension. He lifted his hand. "Everything good?"

Trent handed him the pizza. "I'll tell you about it when we get inside."

They entered the house, Pammie trailing behind. Then she rushed into her room and slammed the door. If it weren't for the fact that he knew Pammie's tantrum wouldn't last, he would go after her. She would be back to her cheerful self in about ten minutes, he assured himself.

"What was that all about?" James asked, turning off the TV and joining him in the kitchen.

Trent found the pizza slicer and started cutting into the pie. "I had a meeting with Pammie's school. They wanted to discuss transition. Said it's time I think about Pammie getting her own place. Live with others like her in a home with caretakers."

James picked up a slice. "Did you tell them you are willing to care for her yourself?"

"I sure did, but they advised me that Pammie would thrive in that quasi-independent environment. It would give her a chance to date. To be with others with Down's syndrome, who understood her. As if I don't know what my sister needs. As if I didn't spend the last few years of my life taking care of her." Trent had left the meeting upset and on the defensive. It was like they had believed Pammie being with him wasn't good enough.

"Nothing beats the love of family," Dontae said, jabbing a finger on the countertop. He reached for a slice.

James patted—more like thumped—his back. "They meant well." He wiped his face with the back of his hand and reached for another slice.

"They created problems. Now, all of a sudden, I'm not good enough. Pammie wants to spend the night at Emily's house. I've never even met her. I'm not sending my sister to some random stranger's house." He flailed his arms. "And what does she know about dating?"

"Bruh, calm down," Dontae said, finally taking another slice. "I think you're taking this too personal. What if something were to happen to you? Who would Pammie have? It's not like you're married or she has other siblings…"

Dontae's questions cut him to the core. "I don't want to think about that. I don't want to think about death. I'm all about living. Being positive." Trent's chest rose and fell with his words. He had lost his parents. He didn't want to think about any more loss. That's another reason marriage wasn't for him. He couldn't bear the possibility of losing a wife.

"I'm just trying to get you to see where they're coming from," Dontae said.

"We'd take care of her," James said. "If anything were to happen… You know that, don't you?"

Pammie came back into the room and they dropped the conversation. Trent used that opportunity to retrieve the second pizza and put the final one in the coal-fired grill. The rest of the night, Pammie entertained them with launching her TikTok channel, singing songs from *Frozen* and other Disney movies.

But Dontae's questions haunted him.

Trent churned on them most of the night. In the morning, it broke his heart to admit that, without him, Pammie had no one, no other recourse, and the fault was no one's but his own.

Chapter Ten

His eyes refused to be redirected. They kept making their way back to Selena, roaming over her body in that black dress and those sexy stilettos with salacious delight. Not a single curve was left hidden, and his eyes feasted on every single one.

Trent leaned against the bar and studied Selena as she danced with her friend, Nadine, under the spotlight. Her body movements were more like planned seduction. His eyes enjoyed every swing of the pendulum. Every time she raked her hands through her curls, he groaned.

Selena had breezed into the Lounge with the confidence of a siren, her violet lips widening in a smile when she spotted him. She had strutted over with those never-ending legs and Trent's voice box had closed. He had never seen his cohost in anything but muted colors, and she had shocked his senses. He had barely recovered before James glided over, forcing him to make introductions. Then James had taken command, flirting with the two women, ignoring Trent's glare.

The women preened and giggled at James's teasing. Trent had observed Selena's reaction from under his lashes, his tension loosening when he didn't see her show interest.

Now he stood nursing his drink and watching the men circle the two women like piranhas around their prey. Most took the hint that the women didn't want to be bothered, but there were a few who didn't get the message. That's why he had declined any invitations to the dance floor. He needed to keep watch.

Just in case.

A man rested his hand on Selena's shoulder. She sidestepped him, but the dude was insistent. He pulled on her small purse and Selena slapped his hand away. Then the man's hand found its way down her back. Both Selena and Nadine appeared to be yelling at the man. Plopping his own drink on the counter and settling his tab, Trent decided it was time for an intervention.

He meandered through the throng and stormed into the middle of the dance floor. Trent grabbed the man and shoved him. "Can't you see the lady doesn't want to be bothered?"

"What's it to you?" he asked, getting into Trent's space, his breath filled with strong liquor.

Trent's lip curled. "Get out of here before I throw you out." He couldn't keep his disgust from his tone.

"It's okay," Selena said, tapping him on the shoulder. "Trent, you don't have to do anything."

"Kick his butt," Nadine encouraged, her eyes flashing with amusement. Trent had a feeling she was laughing at him, like she knew he was jeal— He wasn't jealous. He was looking out for his co-host. One who had no idea of her effect on the men in the club.

"Quit encouraging him," Selena said to Nadine before facing him. Her forehead was lined with sweat and her chest heaved from dancing. She looked delectable. When he saw the man's eyes on Selena's body, his tongue licking his lips, Trent's fists curled. Then he registered the cell phones pointed their way, onlookers ready to press Record.

James marched over. "Go cool down," he commanded, his brow furrowed. "I'll handle him."

The deejay put on a tune to hype up the crowd and their attention diverted from the melee.

"He's not worth it," Selena whispered, grabbing Trent's hand. "Don't forget, we're on duty. The talent comes on in another hour. Let's just chill until then. You don't want to end up with an arrest or a lawsuit because of a sorry drunk." She dragged him to the VIP section and plopped onto the couch. "I needed to get off my feet anyway. It's been a while since I went clubbing. Or had fun. But my feet are protesting."

Trent nodded but kept his eyes on James and Nadine. He watched the pair usher the obnoxious man out of the building. Only then did he relax.

"I would have handled it," Selena said, looking unbothered. "He was a nuisance, but he wasn't a threat. I wasn't helpless or in need of rescuing."

He clenched his jaw. "You didn't see how dude was looking at you. I won't apologize for confronting that perp. He was looking at you like he…"

She curled her body toward him, her hands touching her delicate throat. "Like he what?"

Trent pinned her with a gaze. "Like he wanted to have you for dessert."

Selena gasped, covering her mouth with her hand. "What did you just say?" she whispered, her voice velvety from the connotation of Trent's words. The music blasted in the background, but she wouldn't have been able to tell the song playing if asked. The man next to her had her full attention.

His eyes darkened. "You heard me. I didn't stutter." His voice had dropped, as well.

It was like they were the only two people in the room.

She twirled her curls. "I was just having fun. Dancing with a friend."

"I saw." Trent's eyes raked her body before he said, "So did every other man in here."

There was no mistaking the mutual desire, the tension arising between them. Selena struggled to keep up with this newfound awareness. This was her coworker. A man known for his prowess with the ladies. She couldn't let her Cinderella moment delude her into thinking this was something more. Not that she wanted...something more.

She scoffed. "They're taken with my clothes. With how I look. How many of them would notice me or find me appealing if they saw me in my regular work gear?"

"I would." He cleared his throat and leaned to whisper in her ear, "I have."

Her mouth popped open and she put some distance between them. She would admit she liked being found desirable but she couldn't get caught up. She was dealing with a man who had a Ph.D. in flirting and she reminded herself that Trent could be teasing her. He had the gift of gab...a talented tongue, if the rumors were to be believed. A rumor she was now very interested in investigating for its veracity.

"I don't know if I believe that..." She wet her lips and Trent's eyes followed the movement. Her body heated and she resisted the urge to fan herself.

"I know I have a reputation, but I'm not in the business of lying to women. I'm open with what I want. Any woman who wants to be with me knows what she is getting into and gladly agrees." He had the nerve to give a smile, showing his beautiful teeth. "Satisfied customers."

Her brow arched. *My. Oh, my.* A server brought them water and Selena accepted a glass. She needed to cool down. She guzzled the contents, wishing for another kind of cooling.

Just then, Trent's cell buzzed. He pulled out the phone and read the text. In an instant, his demeanor changed. His face was filled with concern.

She stood, running her hands down her sides. "What's going on?"

"I've got to get home. Mindy texted that Pammie is fine but there is some kind of emergency."

"Let me grab my coat." She paused for a beat to see if he would decline her accompanying him, but he nodded and gestured for her to lead the way. She called Nadine but the call went to voice mail so Selena left a quick message saying she was leaving with Trent.

The cool December air slapped her in the face and she welcomed it. This interruption was needed. Inside the cozy cavern of the club, it was easy to get carried away. She was honest enough to admit that she felt mild disappointment their flirting session had ended, but her concern outweighed any disappointment.

Trent beckoned a cab and they jumped inside.

He squeezed her knee. "Thanks for coming with me. I tried calling Mindy, but I didn't reach her, and

I don't allow Pammie to use her phone after eight o'clock," he said in a neutral and distracted tone.

"Of course, I would come. I care about Pammie. And you."

He shot her a glance before giving her a bland smile.

Selena wasn't sure how to read that. She looked out the window. Maybe he regretted flirting with her. Maybe he regretted having her come home with him. She chewed on her lower lip. Or maybe he was worried about his sister and she needed to chill.

Trent wasn't the type who would have a problem telling her he didn't want her there. His cell rang. Mindy had called him back. Her own cell phone pinged with a notification. It was Nadine.

Girl. I got your message. Do you have protection?

It's not like that. He had an emergency.

An emergency only you can fix. Pearl and Pants, girl.

Selena cracked up. You are ridiculous. Did you leave?

Nah. Hanging with James.

Her brows shot up near her forehead. She would grill her friend later for details. OK. Stay safe.

She must have closed her eyes and drifted off because the next thing Selena felt was Trent giving her shoulder a gentle shake.

"I'm sorry. I didn't mean to fall asleep," she said with a loud yawn.

"Okay, Tarzan." Trent chuckled. "Let's get inside." He paid the driver and Selena was surprised when he told the cabbie to wait.

"It's for Mindy," he explained once they were in the elevator. "Her mother had a nasty fall down the stairs. She has osteoporosis."

Mindy was waiting in the hallway, purse in hand. She appeared agitated and incoherent. Selena stepped free of her heels, reached out and held on to Mindy's arms. The minute she made contact, the woman broke into tears. Trent excused himself to check on Pammie, who hovered down the hallway.

"Take a deep breath. Inhale, one…two…three. Then release, two…three…four." Selena walked the other woman through the calming exercises. "Your mother is fine. She is in the hospital. She is safe."

Trent returned and handed Mindy some tissues. "I have a cab waiting for you. Do you need me to accompany you?"

Mindy's lower lip trembled. "No. I'm good. I should be back in a couple days."

"Don't worry about anything. We'll be okay." Trent said. "I'll get Linda from the temp agency to cover, so take as long as you need. You know Pammie is used to her, so concentrate on taking care of your mother. Ms. Wanda will be just fine." After uttering a quick thank-you, Mindy went through the door.

"You were wonderful," Trent said with admiration.

Selena waved a hand. "I didn't do much." She changed the subject. "Where's Pammie?"

"She's washing her face," he said, hiding a smile. "Did you happen to see her face?"

"No. I was too busy with Mindy." She cocked her head. "Why?"

"Why don't you go see? She's in her bathroom." He looked like he was trying to contain his laughter.

She wrinkled her nose and made her way inside Pammie's bedroom and toward the private bathroom. When she saw Pammie, Selena couldn't hold her gasp. Her eyes scanned the bathroom sink, which was cluttered with several lipsticks, eyeliners, eye shadow and rouge. Pammie's cheeks were dotted with large red circles, her eyebrows shaped with jagged blue arches, and her lips were a bright red. Selena would have laughed if it wasn't for the fact that Pammie looked crushed. Her heart melted.

"Trent made me wash it off," Pammie stammered, trying to hold her tears.

"Here, let me help." Selena took one of the wash rags hanging on the towel rack, ran it under warm water, adding soap. "Close your eyes, Pammie." Gently, she cleansed the young woman's face. When she was done, Selena scrubbed the sink and helped her put away the makeup.

"What made you put this on?" she asked once they had returned to Pammie's bedroom. They sat together on the bed.

"I was trying to look nice for Franco and I want to look nice at the winter concert."

"Franco?" Selena repeated, reaching over to touch Pammie's cheek. "Who's Franco?"

Pammie broke into tears and fell into Selena's arms. "He's a boy at school. I like him."

"Oh, Pammie." Selena cuddled the young woman who was very much like a child. Patting her on the head, she said, "How about I show you how to do your makeup another time?" Pammie gave a vigorous nod before kissing Selena on the cheek and asking her to come to her concert the evening of December 19. Selena placed a reminder into her calendar and then stayed until Pammie had fallen asleep. She didn't know how much time passed before she felt a presence behind her.

"How is she?" he asked, standing close enough for her to know he had showered. He smelled like fresh soap...and man. Her body went into high alert.

"I promised her I'd show her how to do her makeup," Selena whispered, gazing down at the beatific smile on Pammie's face.

Trent held out a hand. "Thank you for helping her. I couldn't hold my laughter. I might have hurt her feelings, which is the last thing I want to do."

She loved how he cared for his sister. With Pammie, he was tender. She put her hand in his and felt a shock. A tingle. Trent rubbed his thumb against hers. Then he lifted her hand and placed his lips on her knuckles. It was a light kiss, grazing each one.

She took a jerky breath and broke contact, reclaiming her hand. "I'd better be getting home... I've got a lot of packing to do tomorrow." And she needed to process all of these sensations, get back her equilibrium. This man was wreaking havoc with her common sense. He was everything she told herself she didn't want, but she was having a hard time remembering why.

"Packing?" he asked.

"Yes, I have a buyer for my practice." She shook her head. "My place spent one day on the market. One day. My Realtor told me I was in a prime location, but even he was surprised that we had an offer so soon. Plus, the offer was over the asking price. We close right after the new year."

"But that's close to a month away. Why the rush?"

She shrugged. "My parents drilled into me to never put off for tomorrow what I can do today. So I like to get things done well in advanced."

"I like that thinking because then you won't be scrambling to get things done at the last minute. Well, Congratulations and if you need help, call," he said, his breath minty, his teeth white.

Folding her arms to hide the evidence of her budding desire, Selena nodded, reminding herself that sex with a coworker was the precursor to all kinds of issues and traipsed out of Pammie's room, her eyes pinned to the exit.

Trent caught up to her before she got to the front door. "Thank you for tonight," he said, enfolding her in his arms. He lingered, like he didn't want to let go.

Selena molded her body to his. Tense seconds passed while they stood there. Desire evident but not acknowledged.

He released her. "Let me put on my shoes and walk you down."

"There's no need." She rushed out the words. "You have a twenty-four-hour doorman. I feel quite safe."

"I want to." He slipped his feet into a pair of boots and donned a black wool overcoat.

She nodded and reached for her shoes. Her achy feet protested but it was close to forty degrees outside. She wasn't going to go barefoot and risk catching a cold. They took the elevator down to the lobby and she waited for Trent to hail a cab.

Before she got in, he said, "Let's meet Monday afternoon for lunch. I heard about an amazing girl group who will be performing at the Comedy Scene. We can talk more then."

"Sure," she said, settling inside the cab.

He tapped on the window before the cabbie pulled off. "Guess what," he said. "It's after midnight. You're no Cinderella. You're you. And you're still devastatingly beautiful."

Chapter Eleven

"It's about time you showed your face," were the first words Helen spoke to Selena in three weeks. It was now the twelfth of December and Selena had awakened early that Monday with an ache in her heart. She needed to see her mother, to make sure Helen was all right, and in person since she'd been avoiding her all this time. Selena had entered the Gracie Square Hospital, prepared to insist on a visit with her mom. She couldn't hide her shock when staff told her that Helen had been asking for her. Selena had rushed to her mother's room, experiencing a mix of dread and anticipation.

She opened her mouth to answer but swallowed her snippy retort. Instead, she hugged her mother close. "I missed you, Mom," she whispered, savoring the feel of her mother's arms about her. It had been too long. Helen lifted a hand to cover hers. Tears brimmed in Selena's eyes at the physical contact. She closed her eyes and inhaled her mother's unique scent mixed with lavender. There was no place safer than her mother's arms.

Then Helen stiffened. "It's all your fault."

Selena froze and eased out of the embrace. She knew that tone. Wiping her face, she steeled herself for the impending vitriol, but still tried to divert her mother's attention. "It's a really sunny day outside. Should we put on our coats and go outside for a bit?"

"It's all your fault," Helen repeated with a snarl.

"Can you explain what you mean when you say that?" she asked in a careful, neutral tone. She didn't want her mother shutting down. Something about this conversation made Selena believe her mother was ready to talk. After all these years.

"You made him leave," Helen said, pointing at her. "You were a colicky baby and that's why your father abandoned us."

Selena held on to her temper. Her intuition must be off. She spoke through her teeth. "I was thirteen, Mom. Way past that stage. You and I know why he left and that it had nothing to do with me. Or you."

Helen gave her a look filled with such contempt that she stepped back. "You think you're better than me? You got you some fancy degree and figure you know more than me."

"It's not a matter of being better, Mom," Selena said, placing a hand on her hip. "I'm only stating facts. Dad left because he had another family. The son he always wanted."

"That I couldn't give him because of you," Helen bit out.

Selena touched her chest. This was new. Her mother had never made such an accusation before. Her heart thumped against her chest and her stomach muscles constricted. Inching closer to her mom, she asked, "What do you mean? How is this on me?"

Helen wrapped her arms about herself. Selena took a chance and placed her hand on her mother's shoulder. "Tell me. Tell me why you hate me."

Shrugging off Selena's hand, Helen said, "He wanted a son. I had had a tough pregnancy and an even tougher delivery with you. They ended up having to do a C-section and, after some complication—I don't know what—I couldn't have any more children." Her chin wobbled. "I couldn't give him a son because of you."

"I didn't know you wanted more children," Selena said, twisting her hands. "I'm sorry about that."

In an instant, Helen's sorrow turned into spite. "Yes. You should be sorry. Because that's what you are. Sorry. Sorry. Sorry. I'm sorry the day I had you. It ruined my chances at having the child I actually wanted."

Selena gasped and backed away, her legs threatening to crumble like a sandcastle under the waves.

Helen's cruel words hacked away at her heart as an ax would a tree. She retreated, searching her mother's face for regret. But Helen's eyes told Selena the truth. Her mother had meant her words. Tears trekked down Selena's cheeks and she covered her mouth to keep from breaking out in a sob, to keep her mother from seeing how much her words hurt.

"Get out!" Helen wailed. "Leave me alone." She cut her eyes and turned, shutting out Selena. This time it felt like for good.

She stumbled from her mother's room, clutching her stomach.

Selena kept it together until she got home. But once she made it through the door, she collapsed to the floor. All these years she had treasured her early years with her dad—never questioning when he'd made her play basketball and go camping; never questioning why he hadn't encouraged her to do what he'd called "girly stuff." Her body trembled as she released her ache. Now she knew why Helen treated her the way she did.

The pain hurt like a stab to the gut.

Though a part of her knew it wasn't true, Selena felt...unlovable. Unwanted by both her parents for not being the son they both desired. She cried until she was empty, shivering on the cold marble floor. She would have remained there if she hadn't remembered her lunch date with Trent. Without changing her position, Selena sent Trent a text.

I can't make it.

That was all she had the strength to write. Just that very act sapped her energy. Seconds later, her cell phone rang. She didn't want to answer but knew Trent would call again.

"Yes?" she breathed.

"Selena? Are you okay? What's going on?"

His rapid-fire questions were too much for her to handle. "Nothing. I—I can't. I can't." To her horror, she sniffled, a dead giveaway she had been crying. "I'll see you later at the radio station. Okay?" She pressed End and tossed the phone. She heard it slide across the floor and grunted with satisfaction when it stopped with a thud under the couch. Then she closed her eyes.

"I'm not leaving until you answer the door," Trent called from outside Selena's townhouse. He pounded on the door, determined to continue doing so until she opened it. After her phone call, Trent had gotten two lunch orders to go and raced over to Selena's place. In all their time together, he had never heard his cohost sound so…dejected…defeated… despondent. He knew he couldn't carry on with his day, knowing she was at home crying. If sniffles could break a heart, then his would be broken in several pieces.

He eyed the window over the bush, debating if he should see if it was unlocked. Then he paused.

He was a black man in the snooty Upper West Side. That would be a double *no*. He pressed on the doorbell, intent on annoying her to answer.

"Selena," he yelled. "Let me in."

From the corner of his eye, he saw a curtain in the neighboring brownstone shift and blew out a breath. His chest heaved and his adrenaline was off the scale but he needed to calm down. Appear rational. Non-threatening.

He released a plume of air and leaned on the doorbell. "Please answer. Please. I'm drawing unwanted attention."

The door cracked open and he slumped with relief before pushing his way inside the hallway. He froze. What he saw facing him could be a character from *The Walking Dead.* Her hair was disheveled, her clothes unkempt, and her eyes appeared hollow, swollen. She hadn't just been crying. She had been balling her eyes out.

She stood before him, unblinking, arms hanging by her sides, watching him watch her.

"Are you okay?" he asked, though it was evident she was not. But that was the best starting point he had.

She shook her head. Her eyes rested on the bag in his hands. "What's that? Lunch?" she croaked.

He nodded, holding up the brown bag. "Burgers and fries with bottles of their special iced tea."

She wrapped her arms around herself and shuffled out of the hallway toward the kitchen.

He noticed her phone jutting out from under the couch and picked it up. Then he placed it on the kitchen island and looked around. Her place was large, airy, clean and... He searched for the word— bare. Bare walls. No pictures. Sparse furniture. He had seen hotel rooms with more. Nothing here showed Selena's personality. Nothing said she lived here.

"How long have you been in this house?" he asked, placing the bag on the small table in the kitchen. It had top-of-the-line appliances—just like his. Only hers appeared to have never been used.

"Just over two years," she said.

His mouth dropped open. "You're a minimalist."

She shook her head. "I have stuff. I just never put them up."

"Wasn't this house featured in *Essence*?"

"Yeah. I had it staged. I had them take out everything after the photo shoot."

"You should have kept some stuff."

She shrugged. "I've got...stuff. Tucked in bins in my closet."

Trent went over to the sink to wash his hands. He didn't see any kitchen or paper towels, so he wiped his hands on his pants. Selena was too much in a daze to do more than stare. He proceeded to lay out their lunch then gestured for her to sit. "Eat," he commanded.

She took a tentative bite. Then, as if realizing she was hungry, she chomped down on her meal. Trent followed suit, relieved she had an appetite. That was a good sign.

He reached in the bag for a napkin and wiped his mouth. "What's up? Talk to me."

Selena looked him in the eyes and all he saw was sorrow. Pain. "Did you ever want to know something really bad but when you got the answer, you realize you would have been better off not knowing?"

"Huh?"

"I saw my mother today and she told me some things that messed me up. She's been saying how much she hates me for years. Now I understand why." Her voice broke.

Trent reached over to take her hand. He wanted to hold her, to tell her that wasn't the truth, but he knew he had to listen. His mother had loved him with the fierceness of a mama bear. He couldn't imagine a mother being anything less.

"You heard the story about my father leaving," she said, scraping the chair back to stand, her food forgotten. "After his departure, my mother changed. She became a different person. I think her mental illness was always there, lurking, until heartache brought it to the surface. Gone was the wonderful mother who used to comb my hair, bake me cookies. There were days where she never uttered a word. Not one word. It was like I wasn't there."

His heart twisted at the isolation Selena must have felt.

"Then when she spoke, I regretted hearing her

voice. Over time, my mother became verbally abusive toward me, blaming me." She walked over to the window and Trent joined her. "All these years, I didn't get why she hated me. Why she loathed being in my presence. I didn't understand what I had done to deserve such bad treatment."

"You were a child and she was wrong to blame you," Trent said, his anger building.

"She doesn't see it that way." Selena pointed to her chest. "Because of me, she couldn't have more children. She had some kind of complication during childbirth. My mother says that's why Daddy left, because she couldn't give him the son he wanted." Her voice cracked, whipping at Trent's heart. "When he got his son, with another woman, he left without any remorse, any guilt. I took care of my mother as best as I could. But even there I failed her. I had to place her in a mental institution five years ago and she resented me for it. Said I deserted her. I was afraid to leave her alone because I wasn't sure…" She trailed off but Trent understood what she couldn't say. "That's why I became a therapist, so I could help her. I help so many people, but nothing I do for my own mother is good enough."

"I'm so sorry, Selena. Both your parents are selfish and their actions are reprehensible," Trent said. "You should have been a regular teenager but you had to take on caring for your mother like you were the adult. It was too much, too soon and I'm surprised you didn't end up on the streets or something worse."

She sniffled and faced him. "I grew up under the weight of being unwanted. My father, whom I idolized, didn't want me. My mother didn't, either. I know I sound pitiful but it makes me wonder if I'm unlovable."

Her confession tore at his gut and the crack in his heart widened. Trent moved close and touched her arm. "You're not unlovable." He curled his fists to keep from grabbing her into his arms. He didn't want to scare her with the intensity of the emotions coursing through his body. He spoke through gritted teeth, his fury boiling within. "Your mother being mentally ill does not excuse her deplorable behavior. I might be wrong for saying this, but God knew why He didn't give her more children. But your father could use an introduction to my fists. You need to confront that lowlife. He's a class-A jerk. His selfishness was the beginning of your pain."

"I can't," she whispered, her shoulders slumping.

"Why?" His chest heaved.

"You don't know how much I wish I could confront him. Yell at him, but it's not possible." She wiped her face and squared her shoulders. Then she told Trent something that released all his anger like air coming out of a balloon. In a voice crushed with grief, Selena said, "I was thirteen years old when my father walked out of the door. I will never see him again. Seven months after his departure, my father died. He was at the Twin Towers when they collapsed, September 11."

Chapter Twelve

Makeup was the magic of the gods.

Selena stood in her bathroom in her underwear and nude pantyhose, scrutinizing her face, amazed that a few strokes could conceal the effects of her crying earlier that day. After her revelation, Trent had scooped her into his powerful arms, taking her to sit on her love seat. He had cuddled her close to his chest and urged her to rest, whispering soothing words. She thought she'd felt his lips brushed the top of her head but she couldn't be too sure. Selena had relaxed against him, frightened at how right it felt having him there with her, accepting his comfort, inhaling his scent, before eventually falling asleep. It had been hours before she had awakened to find herself in bed.

Alone.

Trent had scrawled a note telling her not to come into the radio station. He would get a stand-in. A first for her. She had never missed a night but Selena had been too exhausted to put up a fuss. He had suggested that they could meet at the comedy club tonight, if she were up to it.

She had texted him for the address before finishing her half-eaten meal. The burger had been cold but it had appeased her growling stomach. Then she had dressed in the teal number and slipped on the gold heels.

Eyeing herself in the mirror, she patted her curls, which she would leave loose. "Admit it. You like him."

She shook her head.

"You like him," she said with a little more force. "Be honest with yourself."

She groaned and flailed her arms. "Fine. I like him." She strutted out the bathroom, careful not to teeter in her heels, and grabbed her purse and coat. Securing the locks on her town house, Selena noticed her neighbor peering through the window and gave a wave. She had seen the elderly man many mornings, but he never spoke or greeted her. The curtains slid back into place. One day, she was going to knock on his door and introduce herself.

Hailing a cab, she forgot about her neighbor as soon as she got in and gave the driver the address for the comedy club. The cabbie swerved through the streets with skill and precision. Selena closed her eyes and settled into the seat, trying to recall what it had been like being in Trent's arms, savoring the flex of his strong muscles and abs, his long fingers stroking her thumb. She had been too distraught to register all he had been doing, how it had felt, but her body remembered. Trent was not the man she believed him to be. He was nothing like the man she had called "Dad" for thirteen years. In fact, to compare the two men would be an insult to Trent. He was a tease but he was gentle and kind.

He was…more.

More than she had thought.

More than she'd expected.

She bit her lower lip. *Ugh.* She wanted more, but she didn't know if the feeling was reciprocated. He had been nice enough to help a friend and she, starved for attention, was reading more into their friendship than she should. A horn blared and her eyes popped open. The traffic had slowed to a snail's pace. Glancing at the map on her watch, Selena could see she was going to be about twenty-three minutes later than predicted.

Twenty-three long minutes until she saw him again. Patience was needed. Admission of how much she liked him, being in his presence, getting his attention, was followed with anticipation. Anticipation of sharing a meal, of hearing the low rumble of his voice in her ear, or perhaps the press of his lips…on hers. She touched her lips and exhaled.

She was getting carried away.

And she shouldn't.

It was ridiculous, really. Getting worked up because of a generous gesture from the opposite sex. Ridiculous, yet here she was doing just that.

Something plopped on the window. Her brows furrowed. Wait. Was that snow? The weather hadn't said anything about the possibility of snow. She eyed her feet and bit back a groan.

"It's just a few flurries, Ms. Cartwright. It won't settle. You and your shoes will be fine," the cabdriver said, startling her. She thought she detected a light Jamaican accent.

Touching her chest, she asked, "You know my name?" And why was he all in her business instead of keeping his eyes on the road?

"Everybody knows who you are," the tiny man chuckled. "I listen to your show every evening. I have to support my fellow yardie."

"Yeah, man," she replied, easing into the West Indian vernacular.

He asked about the last time she'd visited Jamaica and Selena was ashamed to admit she hadn't been back in close to twenty years.

"I go every year," he said. "My auntie lives in Montego Bay."

Selena smiled. "I'm going back soon."

"Yes. Make sure you live it up and stay at the Iberostar. It's one of the best resorts on the island." He pulled up to the club and used that moment to ask for her number. She tipped him well but declined. Reason one: she spotted the ring on his left hand. Reason two: he was way too short for her. Reason three: her heart and mind seemed intrigued by... someone else. But she was flattered and told the cabbie so. He took her rejection with a grin, and a good-natured shrug typical of most Jamaican men.

"All right, love. Keep sweet. Take my card. Call me if you need a ride home." Blowing her a kiss, he merged into traffic.

She placed the business card in her purse, more than happy to support a fellow Jamaican. Maybe she would give him a shout-out on the air. Then, tucking her purse under her arm, she went in search of Trent.

After their tender moment earlier in the day, she was more than ready to see his face—and that sexy smile that made her feel like he only had eyes for her. She checked her coat and meandered through the crowd, her eyes searching. Yearning. Soft music played in the background but Selena wouldn't have been able to name the song.

Then she saw him. And that smile.

Only it was trained on the four leeches—er, women—seated around him in the booth.

Goodness. She was wearing that dress.
And those heels.
They weren't fit for anywhere but the bedroom.
From where he sat in the curved booth, Trent could see the other men ogling Selena as she marched

toward him, her purse, swinging at her side. He had arrived a few minutes' early to secure a booth and wait for Selena. But his presence had attracted the attention of four sorority sisters in the booth next to him. He knew they were sorority sisters by their green-and-pink bags with Greek lettering. Trent had given them a wave and offered to cover their tab for the night. The women took his gracious act as a signal to join him.

Trent had been polite, engaging in conversation, but keeping his eyes trained on the door for Selena's appearance. And what an entrance she had made. He nodded to something one of the women said, but from under his lashes, he watched Selena. The swell of her hips, those juicy thighs and that tiny waist. He was pretty sure his hands could span them. Oh, would he love to find out if he was right.

She drew close and he almost groaned at the sight of her luscious lips painted a ruby-red. Gone was the woman curled against him with doubt. In her place stood a confident, sexy avenger. With a toss of her hair, she asked, "Can you make room for me?" and raised her eyebrow as if she expected him to move at her command.

A couple of the women glanced over Selena's body with jealousy in their eyes. He held back a grin before he did what she wanted. Move.

Trent gave them a lopsided grin. "Ladies, it's been a pleasure. I hope you enjoy the show." He waited for them to scoot over so he could leave. Extricating himself without touching arms or legs was tricky but Trent made sure he didn't make physical contact. Not with Selena's hot gaze pinned on him.

"Thanks for rescuing me," he said once he was by her side. He led her to another curved booth in the far corner of the club.

She bopped him with her purse and perched at the edge of the leather couch, giving him a generous view of her long legs. "You looked like you were lapping up the attention."

He cocked his head. Her tone sounded like she was jealous. But she didn't have a right or reason to be. Then he thought of how he'd felt about the men eyeing her a couple of minutes ago and gave a mental shrug. Trent decided to be honest.

"I was waiting for you. Only for you." He slipped into the booth, scooting close to her.

Slowly, her lips spread into a wide smile and her eyes warmed. "Whatever. I don't believe that."

He cleared this throat. "Well, believe this. You are the hottest woman in here, which makes me the luckiest guy in the world because I get to be seen with you."

Even under the dim light, he could see a red hue rise from her chest to her cheeks. Selena ducked her head with a shyness he found appealing. He signaled a server over and ordered a ginger ale—he was on the job. Selena selected the frozen lemonade with real strawberries. Tapping his fingers on the table, Trent acknowledged this felt more like a date than work. He reminded himself to remember their purpose in being there.

Taking a long sip of her drink, Selena licked her lips. "This is good. I know it's cold out, but this is worth the shivers." She twirled the lemonade with her straw.

"How are you doing?" Trent asked. "I didn't want to leave you, but I had to go into the station."

"Thank you for covering the show for me." She didn't make eye contact. "I feel guilty for unloading on you, but thank you for listening. I've never told anyone about my father's death. It's not something my mother talks about. She refuses to acknowledge that he's gone. That he's gone and never coming back."

"You can't control what your mother does and does not do," he said. "I was glad to be there for you today. I felt honored you felt safe to confide in me."

"It felt good to release. To grieve," Selena said. Then she blew out a breath of air and changed topics. "I did take some time to read over the paperwork you sent on starting the foundation. I'm going to use the same attorneys you used to help me."

He puffed his chest. "I'm glad I could be of help," he said, going along with the flow of conversation. He understood her need to focus on something else than her mother.

"You were. Thank you so much." She glanced around the club. "Tell me what you know about the talent tonight."

"It's a girl group from Brooklyn called Vocalz, with a *z*. They are supposedly the next Xscape, and they are all single."

Her eyes flashed. "They sound like Xscape?"

He nodded. "I listened to a brief clip and they've got some serious skills. They will be performing before the comedians, to get the audience pumped."

"I'm excited," she said, bouncing in her seat. "If they are as good as you say, let's hope they're available Valentine's Day."

Trent kept his eyes on her face, ignoring her heaving chest. If it was anyone but Selena, he would have seen that as a ploy, a calculated move. But this was Selena, a woman who had no idea of her desirability. She sipped on her drink and moaned. Yes, moaned. Trent had to pull his gaze away before he did something crazy like taste those lips to see if they were as delectable as they looked. He noticed a couple men gawking at her and knew it had nothing to do with her celebrity status and everything to do with that straw. He stole a glance her way. Sure enough, she slurped away with delight. Oh, to be that straw covered by those ruby lips. Or that glass she held tightly in her hands.

He emitted a low groan at the images those actions evoked. He wasn't going to sleep well tonight. Trent arched a brow, giving the men a stare down. They turned away and he exhaled. If she was his girl, he might ban her from drinking, or eating, in public. Or feed her on the regular so she'd stop this sensual gorging on food.

The deejay announced the Vocalz. A group of four women, who appeared to be in their early twenties, made their way to the stage. They looked so fresh-faced and innocent, dressed in army-toned jumpsuits and sneakers. Then they began to sing.

His mouth dropped open. Trent looked over at Selena.

Her face was brighter than the fluorescent lights under which they sat. "Wow. Talk about chills." She rubbed her arms. "Goose bumps from the first note."

All he could do was nod. Trent didn't understand why a music exec hadn't scooped up the group.

They started singing, "Who can I run to?" an iconic Xscape number. He and Selena gave each other a high-five. "I think we've found our act."

She bobbed her head. "I agree."

As soon as their performance ended, Trent and Selena made their way backstage. They had no difficulty getting through because of their celebrity status. Vocalz jumped at the chance to perform and, after taking a few selfies and exchanging contact information, Trent and Selena decided to leave.

He helped Selena into her coat and held open the door, gasping at the frigid December air. He found he enjoyed doing those small acts for her, even more now that he was getting to know her. But his touch had become possessive. Every contact sizzled. His fingertips a live wire, leaving mini impressions on her back, her shoulder, her arm. Like he was branding her. A silent signal to the other men around that Selena was unavailable.

His.

Why was that? That was something he would have to process later. While his mind churned, his mouth moved. "Those girls are going to be huge. Let's bring them into the studio to sign the contract and to give our audience a sneak peek."

"That's a great idea." Selena thanked him and stepped through the door. As soon as they were outside, she squealed and jumped up and down. Her coat was open and she had to be cold, but her excitement seemed to surpass any other feeling. "We have a venue and we have an act. Our ball is going to be a huge success. It's all coming together."

She spun around; her arms spread open.

Her shining eyes and wide smile made his breath catch. Before he could exhale, Selena cupped his face with her hands and crushed her lips to his. It took a beat for his mind to catch up. Selena was kissing him. With gusto. In public. She wasn't asking, either. His brain kicked into gear and his body sprang to life. Without breaking contact, Trent snatched her closer, moving under the shadows, hunching his shoulders to shield them from view. Trent pressed his body to hers before prodding her mouth open, thrusting his tongue into that cavern, savoring his first delicious taste.

Chapter Thirteen

Kissing Trent like that in public had been risky. Tempting. Thrilling.

And a mistake.

That's what Selena told herself later that night, scrubbing the makeup off her face. Not that she had regrets. Observing herself in the bathroom mirror, Selena touched her flushed, swollen lips exulting in the tingles she still felt. What a scorcher. She had initiated, but Trent had taken over, devoured, giving her the best kiss of her life. He had kissed her like he had no intention of ever ending, ever breathing.

Whew. Talk about intense.

But that kiss had to be a one-and-done. Having f-u-n had to come with limits. Boundaries. That's why she was home alone and not with Trent. Not that he had invited her to his place or had asked to come to hers. Maybe he had been unmoved by their lip locking and she was the only one obsessing. Or maybe he hadn't wanted to deal with the thorny issue of sleeping with his sidekick.

She picked up her pink electric toothbrush and brushed her teeth to remove the seeds from the frozen strawberries in her lemonade. It wasn't even 10:00 p.m., but she had undressed and slipped into a pair of cotton pajamas, intending to make it an early night. She had to go into her practice tomorrow to finish preparations before the closing date set for January 2 She had hired movers, but Selena wanted to be there to oversee everything.

Selena traipsed into her kitchen to get a glass of water. Her tear fest had left her feeling dehydrated. While she was there, she would grab her Kindle out of her purse. With no clients in the morning, she intended to read one of the many books she had purchased but never found the time to read. Reading would be a distraction, a healthy pastime. She needed to think about something other than her dysfunctional upbringing and that kiss.

She had just poured water in a glass when the doorbell chimed.

Selena had installed a video doorbell but her cell phone was in her purse. Her heart raced. What if Trent had decided to come for more? Touching her lips, she didn't know if she had the strength to turn him down. The bell rang again. She walked over to the door and looked out the peephole. Seeing the top of her bestie's head, she unlocked the door.

"What are you doing here so late?" Selena asked, giving Nadine a tight squeeze and stepping aside for her to enter. "Get in here. It's windy out there."

"It's brick cold. You never answered my texts and I got worried, so I packed an overnight bag and came over after my shift," Nadine said, worry evident in her tone. She took off her coat and handed it to Selena, looking around like she expected someone to jump from behind and attack them. Nadine was still in her scrubs, which meant her friend would be making use of the Jacuzzi in the guest room.

Selena frowned. "You texted? I didn't get any messages."

"Check your phone. You had me thinking you were here passed out or in a hospital somewhere." Nadine's voice reverberated in the large space. She took off her sneakers, dropping them with the other shoes on the mat near the door. She rubbed her hands together and blew into them before she headed for the kitchen. Selena could hear banging around and figured her friend was reaching for the single-cup coffee maker.

Selena opened the closet door and hung Nadine's coat on one of the mahogany wooden hangers. Every time she did that, a line from the classic, *Mommy Dearest,* teased her mind. *No more wire hangers.* After watching that movie, both Selena and Nadine had never used metal hangers. Ever. Holding her chuckle, Selena took her purse off the hook on the back of the door and scrounged around for her cell phone.

There were two text messages from Trent. Are you home? followed with Hello?

She sent a quick affirmative response. Then tapped on Nadine's emoji.

Her mouth dropped. There had to be about ten messages. She frowned. Why hadn't she received any? Selena pressed Nadine's contact information, saw the half moon and removed it. "I silenced you by mistake," she said, scrolling through Nadine's messages. She walked into the kitchen. "Sorry, friend. But I am glad you're here."

Nadine put a K-cup into the coffee maker. "How did things go with your mom?"

Sitting around the barstool, Selena caught Nadine up, beginning with her visit with Helen, the prep work for the foundation and ending with the searing kiss she and Trent had shared. Though Nadine had responded to each conversational thread, she perked up when Selena talked about her lip-locking session.

"So, that's it? You're not going to take things further with him?"

Selena shook her head, going to the fridge to refill her water. "No. That would be a bad idea. I'm not trying to compete for any man's attention or date someone I have to worry about. I told you how he was surrounded by those women when I got in the club."

"He's in the spotlight, just like you. He's going

to attract attention." Nadine held up a hand to stop Selena from responding. "You can't judge him by his gorgeous, chiseled face. You told me yourself how thoughtful he is and what he did at Thanksgiving for the homeless. That's stuff for the movies. There is an authentic man behind that public persona. One who I think is into you as much as you are into him, so why not have some fun?"

"I don't know about sleeping with someone I work with. Things could get… complicated."

Nadine took a sip of her coffee and sighed with satisfaction. "How? You think too much. This man gave you the best kiss of your life. I'm pretty sure he would be able to give you something else…" She waggled her eyebrows. "Something that has always eluded you…the *Something's Gotta Give* moment."

Selena lowered her head, knowing she was blushing. "I wish I had never told you that." She had never experienced an orgasm. An embarrassing but true fact she had confided to Nadine after they had watched that old movie starring Diane Keaton and Jack Nicholson. From then on, the movie title became their code phrase for an orgasm.

Nadine came around to take Selena's hands in hers. "You're missing out. Believe me. It's time you learn what all the fuss is about. None of those other jokers you dated were able to take you there. I'm confident Trent isn't lacking in skills, and you'll finally get to *The Big O*." She released Selena's hands. "Just get what you need and move on."

The idea did have some appeal. She would like to

know what the big fuss was about with an orgasm and she was sure Trent would more than get the job done, so to speak. She cocked her head. "Speaking of getting what you need and moving on, did you hook up with James?" Her friend had been reticent to share any information, which was not like her.

Nadine slid her glance away and tucked her hair behind her ears. "Yeah…we got together." Then she met Selena's eyes. "I'm still seeing him, actually. We've gone out a couple of times. In daylight."

"What? Miss Love 'Em and Leave 'Em has gone beyond the one-night stand?" Selena teased. "It's not like you to not say anything about it."

"Well, James is…different." Nadine had a sheepish look on her face. "He's built like the *Man of Steel* but inside he's all mushy and sweet. You know he surprised me with a bouquet of flowers on the job. Just because he was thinking about me." She touched her chest. "He's just so sweet, and I can't handle it."

Her friend was gushing over the opposite sex and it wasn't because of something physical. Now she took Nadine's hands. "I'm happy for you. This sounds like the start of something good."

"And Trent sounds like the start of *Something's Gotta Give*," Nadine returned with a cackle.

Selena cracked up. "Okay, I'll see where it goes. Here's to the start of something new for the both of us."

"Is Ms. Selena coming?" Pammie asked, holding Trent's hand and craning her body to look into the crowd. "She said she was coming to hear me sing and to help me with my makeup."

He looked at his watch and scanned the area. Angels, stars and snowflakes hung from the ceiling and large cutouts of the nutcracker and drummer boy graced corner aisles. With Christmas six days away on Sunday, most people showed their holiday spirit by wearing red or green and donning Santa hats or reindeer ears.

Spotting Mindy in the second row, Trent gave a small wave. He was so glad she was back for good and that her mother was doing well. Mindy had made a couple of trips to the hospital in Brooklyn. Each time, Trent had sent bouquets of flowers for both her and her mother and had taken care of Ms. Wanda's hospital expenses. He had also increased Mindy's wages because she wouldn't accept money otherwise.

Seeing Pammie's furrowed brow, Trent sought to reassure her. "She'll be here." He just hoped Selena wouldn't arrive fifteen minutes before curtain call.

They were backstage of the auditorium of the School for Unique Populations, an educational center for adults with special needs that Trent was instrumental in funding. Pammie had graduated from a specialized private high school and he had needed somewhere for her to go during the day. The only choices out there had seemed to cater to the elderly, so he'd worked with educators and social workers to create interest programs for special adults in their twenties. Pammie took cooking and singing classes.

There were also computer, arts and theater classes, as well as a transition program, but he wasn't ready for her to move yet. If ever.

A young man walked up to them. He was about Pammie's height and had bright red hair. "Hi, Pammie," he said, rocking back on his heels. The young man had a wide grin on his face. "What do you plan to sing?"

"'R-e-s-p-e-c-t,'" she breathed. She, too, wore a wide grin. And was she batting her eyes at this boy? Trent's brows creased. It jarred him to see his sister flirting. Like she was grown. Er, well she was, but she didn't know anything about being in a relationship.

Trent's stepped between them. "And what is your name?" he asked, placing a hand on one hip.

"Franco. Franco Jones," he said, a mini James Bond impersonator, hair slick, wide smile, holding out his hand and looking up at Trent. "I like Pammie."

"I like you, too." Pammie giggled and placed a hand over her mouth. Then she tossed Trent a glance, begging him to accept Franco. Be nice.

Ignoring the innocence that he saw reflected in the young man's hazel eyes, Trent wrinkled his brow. "Head on back to your parents. Pammie has to get ready." His tone sounded gruff, but Trent didn't care. With a jerky nod, Franco bounced away to join his parents.

Pammie poked out her lip. "Why'd you do that?"

"What?" Trent drew shallow breaths and tried to smile. He spotted Selena and gave a little wave.

His sister jabbed him in the chest. "You were mean to Franco. That wasn't nice at all." He hated seeing her downturned face and knowing he was responsible. But she didn't know boys like he did, and he had to protect her.

"Thanks for coming," he said to Selena once she was within earshot, greeting her with a light kiss on the cheek. He could smell ginger mints on her breath and he breathed in the familiar vanilla scent, noting her lips were coated with gloss. She was wearing the same long camel-colored coat she had worn during their broadcast. It was unbuttoned, displaying the cream blouse and mustard pants from earlier that day. After the broadcast, Trent had made his way to the school and Selena had rushed home to get her makeup and other accessories.

"Ms. Selena! You're here," Pammie said, jumping up and down.

"Mmm-hmm. I told you I wouldn't miss this. Now, let's get you looking like the star you are."

"Yay!" Pammie beamed, her face brighter than the projector lights overhead. "I washed my face like you told me."

"Good. Let's get started." Selena dug into her bag, took out a makeup case, and applied foundation to Pammie's face. Then she began putting on mascara and eyeliner. Trent's eyebrow arched. His sister was looking amazing…and grown. His stomach twisted.

"You look beautiful." Selena smoothed pink gloss

on Pammie's lips. She showed Pammie how to smack her lips.

"Trent scared Franco off and I think he hurt his feelings." Pammie snatched Selena into a hug, resting her head against Selena's chest. Trent shoved his hands in his pants' pocket and admitted he wouldn't mind switching places with his sister.

His lips quirked. "He'll be all right." He had zero ounce of guilt when it came to what was best for Pammie. And what was best was Franco maintaining a distance of six feet from his sister.

Patting the young woman on the back, Selena then raked her fingers through her braids. "Aww, I'm sorry to hear that but I'm sure your brother didn't mean to scare him." She loosened Pammie's tight grip around her waist and raised Pammie's chin. "Right now, you can't let anything distract you. You have a show to do, so you'd better bring it."

"You're right," Pammie said, giving Selena a thumbs-up.

Selena snapped her fingers and dug in her bag. "I almost forgot your costume jewelry." Selena pulled out a glitzy necklace and matching earrings. Once she was finished putting them on, Trent stifled a gasp. His sister looked grown. As in *grown* grown. He felt panic stir, imagining Franco and other boys, even grown men, checking out his sister.

The director called for the students to gather together. After giving them hugs, Pammie rushed over to join the others. Trent knew that was their cue to exit the stage, but first he had to give Franco a warning glare. The young man had been about to stand next to Pammie when he looked over at Trent.

"Wow. Talk about intimidation." Selena shook her head and began walking toward the auditorium. He fell into step with her. The auditorium was filling up with people.

"What?" he asked, unashamed of the satisfaction he felt seeing Franco stand somewhere else. He couldn't be faulted for trying to look out for his sister's interest. They gravitated to a couple of seats on the right of the auditorium since the seats next to Mindy were taken. Her shoulder grazed his and he welcomed the proximity.

"It might not be my place to say, but you're trying to block something you can't prevent."

He scowled. "Care to explain?"

Selena turned to him, causing their knees to meet. "Your sister may have a disability, but she's an adult. With adult feelings and emotions. You've got to accept that."

He scoffed. "She likes to color and play with her Barbie dolls."

"And she likes boys. Franco, in particular. I think she's ready to enter a relationship, go on a date, maybe even experience her first kiss. Does your program assist with that?"

Relationship? Kissing? His sister? His gut twisted. Fear enveloped him and gave his voice a steely edge. "I think you're right. It isn't your place. You know nothing about caring for someone with Pammie's needs. You've been in her life for what? Five minutes? I've been there for two decades. She is an adult in age not in maturity. Any relationship is out of the question. I can't— I mean, she can't handle that. She needs to focus on her singing."

He turned away from Selena just as the lights dimmed, ignoring her wide-eyed shock at his cutting snipe. His heart thumped, urging him to apologize. He knew his words had been harsh—and undeserving. She straightened, shifting away from him, holding her purse close to her chest, like an armor against the hurt Trent's words had caused. His shoulders slumped and he leaned into her ear.

"Listen, I..."

"Save it," she said through her teeth, faced forward, her tone ice-cool. "You've made your wishes clear; *Brother knows best*. No need to talk about it."

This was when, if things were normal between them, he would counter with a joke about the irony of a therapist shutting him down, but Trent knew Selena wouldn't see the humor. The kiss between them had changed their normal.

Besides, his mind whirled on something she said. *Brother knows best*? Her play on words made him visualize the mother from the Disney film, *Tangled*. The villain. Her infamous song "Mother Knows Best." Because of Pammie, he could recite the lyrics upon request. His left eye twitched. The nerve! Pammie wasn't locked in a tower. She lived in a penthouse. Her bedroom was twice the size of some New York apartments. He gave her everything she wanted. How dare Selena compare him to that monster? He gripped the wooden armrest, his knuckles tight. His chest rose and fell along with his staccato breaths.

Meanwhile, Selena crossed her ankles and, from his peripheral, she appeared at eased and relaxed. Her snapback was on point. Trent had to give Selena that. He cleared his throat to get her attention. He had to address that comparison to Mother Gothel.

Just then, the curtains opened, signaling the beginning of the show. He settled into his seat and forced his attention on the children, the different acts. He clapped and cheered, doing his best to ignore the woman next to him.

Then it was Pammie's turn.

The crescendo of the opening notes to Aretha's song filled the auditorium. When Pammie made her entrance and sang, "Respect," he felt the heat of Selena's side-eye. The unspoken jab. Trent drew in a breath before deciding to concentrate on Pammie. The next time Selena glanced his way, he'd be cool, composed, and completely unbothered.

Chapter Fourteen

Selena wasn't buying Trent's game face or the calm exterior he projected as he stood beside her, swaying to Pammie's song. Selena was trained to read nonverbal cues. His flared nostrils. The jutted jaw. The slightly bunched fists. All signs that her barb had pierced him.

As it should.

Trent was the one who was scared of relationships and he was making the same assumption of his sister. Selena hadn't missed his slip earlier. Or rather, his confession. He'd self-corrected but the truth once spoken was hard to retract. Or ignore.

The professional in her understood his reaction but Selena, the woman, was miffed at how he had spoken to her. All because he refused to accept that his sister was a grown woman. A woman with special needs who desired companionship. Selena took in how Pammie's dress hugged her curvy frame. Pammie needed the chance to explore and embrace womanhood in a healthy way, with Trent guiding her, but he was too stubborn—or scared—to see that.

Nearing the end of her song, Pammie threw her head back and held the note. Selena threw up her hands and egged Pammie on. The crowd went wild, jumping to their feet and clapping their hands. Trent pumped his fists in the air and let out a huge whoop as the music faded. Selena stole a glance his way, struck by the love reflected on his face for his sister. His lashes appeared spiky as he dabbed at the corners of his eyes.

Any ill feeling at him telling her to mind her business dissipated. Even though he was wrong—dead wrong—Trent was coming from a place of love. And she respected that.

Selena placed a hand on his biceps. He swung to face her, placing a hand over hers and giving it a light squeeze.

I'm sorry, he mouthed.

"I get it," she whispered.

It was time for the next act, so they took their seats. His hands linked with hers in the darkened space and her heart skipped a beat. It actually paused for a millisecond. She touched her chest, feeling the rapid pacing under her palm. Her fingers tingled where they connected. Selena welcomed the sensation. It made her feel alive. Present.

That vibe stayed with her for the rest of the ninety-minute concert. Especially since Trent kept their hands joined even while they were congratulating Pammie on her success. After the finale, Trent had surprised all the performers with roses—a gesture that warmed Selena's heart all the way until Trent hailed her a Town Car and jumped in beside her. He closed the door, shutting out the frigid temperatures.

Her mouth dropped. "Where are you going?"

"I'm making sure you get home."

"Um, there's no need for that. And what about Pammie?"

"Mindy texted me during the show to say she would stay over to give me and my lady friend some time."

Selena's brow raised. "'Lady friend'?"

He gave her a light jab. "She's never seen me with a woman around Pammie, so she made that assumption."

"And you didn't correct her?"

"No…" His voice dropped. "Should I have?"

Their eyes met. Then she shrugged and lowered her lashes.

"Don't get all shy with me now." He lifted her chin. "Look at me."

She did. A light shiver coursed through her and she knew it had everything to do with the man next to her. She fought the desire by addressing his earlier behavior. "I didn't like the way you came at me this evening when I meant well." Her voice was supposed to sound firm, instead it sounded…breathy. Flirty, even.

He turned on the interior lights. "You're right and I'm sorry." Trent's eyes darkened, proving her suspicions that her body was speaking a contradictory language from the words coming out her mouth. He reached for her hair and twirled it around his fingers before switching off the lights. He scooted closer in the darkened car and cupped the back of her head. Her toes curled and her chest heaved, anticipating.

A finger outlined her lips before his mouth followed. It was a tender exploration. A quick, chaste taste. Then he pulled away.

Selena wasn't having that. This was the second time she'd had to take the initiative. In a bold move, she straddled him.

"Whoa," he said, grabbing on to the handle.

"That's the smartest thing you've done all night." She nipped at his ear, chuckling at his groan, simultaneously shuddering at the low hum of his voice resounding in her ear. Then he kissed the same spot, and she welcomed the feel of his hips shooting upward. His hands snaked under her coat and tugged her blouse out of her pants before wrapping his arms around her. A light snap.

Deft.

Trent loosened her bra. Expert move. He splayed his large hands on her back. She arched her body

Get up to 4
FREE FABULOUS BOOKS
in your welcome box!

To thank you for being a loyal reader we'd like to send you up to 4 FREE BOOKS, absolutely free when you try the Harlequin Reader Service.

Just write "YES" on the Loyal Reader Voucher and we'll send you your welcome box with 2 free books from each series you choose plus free mystery gifts! Each welcome box is worth over $20.

Try **Harlequin® Special Edition** and get 2 books featuring comfort and strength in the support of loved ones and enjoying the journey no matter what life throws your way.

Try **Harlequin® Heartwarming™ Larger-Print** and get 2 books featuring uplifting stories where the bonds of friendship, family and community unite.

Or **TRY BOTH and get 2 books from each series!**

Your welcome box is completely free, even the shipping! If you continue with your subscription, you can look forward to curated monthly shipments of brand-new books from your selected series, always at a discount off the cover price! Plus you can cancel any time.

So don't miss out, return your Loyal Readers Voucher today to get your Free Welcome Box.

Pam Powers

LOYAL READER
FREE BOOKS VOUCHER
WELCOME BOX

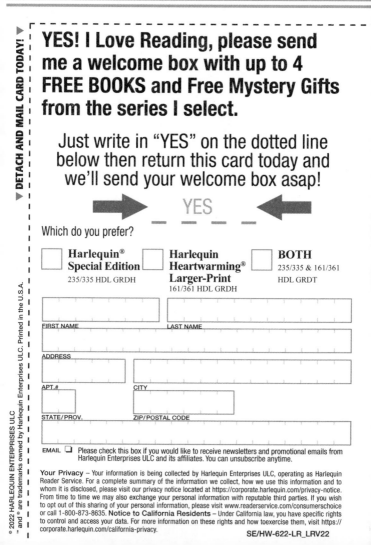

▼ DETACH AND MAIL CARD TODAY! ▼

YES! I Love Reading, please send me a welcome box with up to 4 FREE BOOKS and Free Mystery Gifts from the series I select.

Just write in "YES" on the dotted line below then return this card today and we'll send your welcome box asap!

➡ _ YES _ ⬅

Which do you prefer?

☐ **Harlequin® Special Edition**
235/335 HDL GRDH

☐ **Harlequin Heartwarming® Larger-Print**
161/361 HDL GRDH

☐ **BOTH**
235/335 & 161/361
HDL GRDT

FIRST NAME | LAST NAME

ADDRESS

APT.# | CITY

STATE/PROV. | ZIP/POSTAL CODE

EMAIL ☐ Please check this box if you would like to receive newsletters and promotional emails from Harlequin Enterprises ULC and its affiliates. You can unsubscribe anytime.

SE/HW-622-LR_LRV22

and shielded them with her coat. Seeking. He buried his head into her chest and, within seconds, undid her buttons.

That movement triggered her internal panic button. Her brain screamed for her to stop. To cease this spontaneous back seat make-out session. To think of the driver up front. But the rear windows and partition were both tinted and Trent was doing wonderful things.

Bold.

She clamped her jaw. His tongue then worked magic that drowned out the sounds of the honking horns, the speeding traffic.

Closing her eyes, Selena moaned as he drove her insane. He was so...patient. It was excruciating and delightful, awakening a wildness, a craving she didn't know she possessed. Oh, how she liked it. Her head lolled.

Daring.

Then cool air. It took a second for her process that Trent was buttoning her blouse. Tucking it into her pants, he placed both hands on her hips before lifting her off his lap.

"We've arrived," he said before opening the door and getting out.

She gasped and placed a hand over her mouth. She had been so caught up that she hadn't realized the Town Car had stopped moving. Grabbing her purse, she ducked her head and stepped out.

Mortified, Selena kept her gaze pinned on Trent,

her body turned away from the driver. She couldn't make eye contact, standing there like a zombie while Trent handed the man his card.

"Wait for me and keep the meter rolling," he commanded the man before placing a hand on Selena's back.

That gesture made her remember her actions in the Town car. Keeping her head and posture straight, Selena ambled up the stairs and unlocked her front door. She stepped into the foyer and turned on the lights.

With a swoop, she found herself in Trent's arms, his lips pressed against hers. Their tongues dueled, reigniting her passion.

Something's Gotta Give... Those words teased her mind. She could ask him to stay. Get her to that moment of ecstasy. All she had to do was say the words and Trent would hoist her in arms and— *No.* This situation was too murky. Trent was her cohost and she needed to stop this...madness. Her desire wasn't stronger than her common sense. Besides, Trent wasn't about the long term. She pushed at his chest and Trent broke the kiss.

They both struggled to catch their breaths. He studied her for a few seconds before he stepped back. "I sense you're not ready."

She wet her lips and shook her head, her shoulders squaring. "I don't know if I'll ever be." She tensed, hoping Trent wouldn't be offended or see her as a tease. After all, she was the one who had sprung onto his lap, practically calling him dumb for not making a serious move. And now that he had, she questioned her ability to have such carefree fun without getting attached.

"I'm good with whatever you feel." He touched her cheek, his eyes tender.

Her brow knit and she gripped her coat closed. "You're not upset?"

"My mother raised me right. Taught me about a woman's prerogative. I respect your ability to make a choice and to change your mind."

Her admiration for Trent grew at those words. So did her desire. The fact that he appeared to mean them multiplied it.

Relief made her shoulders relax. "Thanks, Trent. I'll see you tomorrow."

His lips curled. "Our last show for the season. Don't be late." Selena and Trent were hosting a special two-hour broadcast starting at nine the next morning before the *Weeknights with Trent and Selena Show* went on a brief hiatus. The network would air repeats until they returned in the new year and debuted their expanded hours.

The usual hosts for that time slot had been given an early start to their vacation to accommodate this change.

"I won't be," she replied.

With a nod, he slipped through the door.

Selena applauded her decision until she was alone under the covers that night. The thought that she could have been screaming from pleasure kept her awake. Wanting. She wondered if Trent was awake or if he had sought release in another woman's arms. Jealousy flickered. She blinked, hating the thought of someone else dousing the flame she had started. *Ugh.* She pushed that possibility out of her mind. That didn't seem like the Trent she was getting to know. Although, her father hadn't seemed like the type who would leave, either. She had thought he was the best daddy in the world, so maybe she wasn't a good judge of character. Whatever. Selena set her alarm for five-thirty a.m.

Her last thoughts before falling asleep was that she would redirect her energies on the sale of her practice.

The appraisal process was complete and Selena was walking away with a nice sum at the closing. A sum she planned to put toward her mother's care. Thinking of Helen, she pushed back the guilt of not visiting, of not spending the holidays with her mom. Nadine had suggested they plan a mid-week staycation at a five-star hotel and then celebrate Christmas with her parents. Selena had booked their suite and was looking forward to getting a massage. She also booked several spa sessions. That was the only kind of fun that she needed. The more she remembered that, the better off she would be.

Trent made his money from being a words man but if he had to choose a word to describe how he was feeling at the moment, he wouldn't be able to produce one. And it had nothing to do with him and everything to do with the beautiful, enticing woman across from him. Selena kept shifting her gaze away from his, like she was too embarrassed to look him in the eyes.

Like she was trying to forget what had happened last night in the Town Car, when all he wanted to do was remember.

Her full lips. Her wide hips. Her unique scent.

She was intoxicating. A blend of hot and sweet that made him crave more, not less.

But from the time Selena had arrived, she had treated him...normal. No secret smile, no smoldering looks just for him.

Instead, it was as if their rendezvous had been no big whoop while he had tossed and turned all night wanting her arms around him, wanting her in his bed. Well, he didn't like it. Not at all. Not one bit. Oh, she was subtle with it and someone who didn't know her wouldn't pick up on her discomfort, but he knew her. He noticed how her legs were turned away from him, how she made sure their hands didn't touch, and it rankled.

And he wouldn't hesitate to tell her about herself as soon as they were off the air. She was wearing her usual muted tones but it was a fitted dress that she'd accessorized with bold, chunky jewelry and pumpkin-colored lipstick.

Laughing on cue as Selena chatted with a listener, Trent made sure his hand grazed hers when he reached for the ginger mints she had brought to share with him. She sucked in her breath, tripping over her words while on air. Trent covered for her faux pas by providing details on the venue and the lead act they had found for the Valentine's Mingle for Singles Ball.

"Keep sending in your requests," Selena chimed in. "We'll be notifying four hundred fortunate listeners that you get to come party with us." The deejay put on a funky beat. Selena lifted her hands in the air and gyrated her body. The camera crew captured that moment to drop on social media and Trent was sure their online followers were going to make that post go viral. Heck, he planned to check it out himself once the show was over.

Trent peeled his eyes away from her delectable frame and spoke into the microphone. "A Crying Heart, we're still hoping to hear from you again. Our producer has alerted the call line to put you directly through to us. So pick up the phone because Selena and I plan to roll out the VIP treatment for you. After all, your letter inspired this whole shindig."

Even with all their pleading, Trent and Selena had been unsuccessful in getting A Crying Heart to contact the station. It would be a tremendous ratings boost if she called in or showed up to the dance.

"Yes, A Crying Heart," Selena said, "please reach out. I'd love to talk with you."

Her calm compassionate tone took them off the

air and reminded Trent why he enjoyed working with her…and doing other things.

"And that's a wrap," Carla announced. "Go home, people."

As soon as she spoke those words, there was an exodus from the crew. Those who didn't leave were preparing to by packing up. The staff had time off to recuperate and spend time with family. A handful would take shifts to air past episodes and keep track of the fan mail. He heard the chatter of their plans but his eyes were fixed on his cohost. She stood, her bag on her shoulder, and massaged her temples before finally looking his way. "Hey." She lowered her eyes, her cheeks flushed.

"Can we talk?" he asked, scooting closer.

"Yeah. But not here."

Trent nodded. "Okay, where?"

She cocked her head. "Let's go to your dressing room." She pulled on her dress and fretted her bottom lip. "I don't think that would cause suspicion. I mean we work together. It's expected that we would conference. Right?"

"Selena, we're both consenting adults. We didn't do anything wrong." He kept his voice low and lead her to his room. As soon as the door closed, he snatched her into his arms and kissed her. Before she could protest, he broke the kiss. "Sorry, I just needed to get that out of the way. Now, what did you want to talk about?"

"Us?" She gestured her hand between them. "What's happening here?"

He frowned, unsure of what she was asking of him, but then he decided to be honest. "We're exploring. Getting to know each other. Nothing deep." That was the best response he could come up with.

She rocked back on her heels. "Right. Right. I can do that. This doesn't have to be serious and complicated."

Relief seeped through him. "Yes. We can keep things light. A harmless flirtation between two people that like each other."

"Yeah," she breathed out, giving him a bright smile. "F-u-n."

"Cool. We're living in the moment. No matter what happens, we have respect for each other, and I'm sure we will always be able to maintain a good working relationship."

She grabbed his head and nodded. "I agree." Then she sprinkled tiny kisses all across his face. "Since we're both in agreement, we won't have to worry about ruining our work relationship. I don't know why I was so concerned."

Trent quashed the conversation by kissing her until they were both breathless. Hungry for another taste, he lowered his head. Then his phone rang. It was Pammie's school. Holding up a finger, Trent placed another finger over Selena's reddened lips and then answered the call. What he heard made him head out the door, tossing over his shoulder, "Come with me."

She would have taken offensive at his tone, if he hadn't paused and given her look of desperation. "Please."

Chapter Fifteen

Sitting in one of the two chairs outside the principal's office, Selena cocked her head to try to hear what was going on inside. During the ride over when she'd asked what was going on, Trent's only reply had been to shake his head. His jaw had been clamped shut and, apart from squeezing her hand in his, he hadn't uttered word.

Her heart had raced the entire way, unsure of what to expect.

Then when they arrived, Principal Greene had ushered Trent into his office. Since she wasn't family, Selena had taken a seat. It had been thirty long minutes and the door remained closed. She clutched her bag close, having played the *New York Times*'s Wordle of the day, scanning her social media sites, and looking at the amenities for the hotel and had already checked-in, opting to use her phone as a digital key. Now that she was done with that, Selena focused on the kiss between her and Trent.

Closing her eyes, she moistened her lips, trying to recall what it felt like being in his arms, inhaling the scent of his Millésime Impérial Creed. Selena knew this was his favorite cologne and that he kept a bottle in his dressing room for special occasions. The fruity scent on his neck teased her senses and her nose would love to explore his body to find out where else he had sprayed it. That wanton thought made her place a hand on her chest. Who was she turning into because of messing with this man?

The door opened and Pammie stomped out, her face blotched with tears. When she saw Selena, she paused. Trent walked out, his face forceful like thunder, and stormed, "Let's go."

Pammie remained rooted. "I don't want to go to another school."

"This isn't about what you want." Trent spoke through his teeth. "This is about what's best for you."

Pammie folded her arms and raised her chin. Selena looked between them as brother and sister squared off. Neither one looked ready to back down.

Selena jumped to her feet, intending to mediate when she saw Franco and two people, she assumed to be his parents, venture from the office. She felt her eyes go wide as understanding dawned. Something must have happened between Pammie and

Franco. *Oh, boy.* The mother gave her a tentative smile but her husband's face twisted with displeasure. The family scurried down the hallway toward the elevator.

Pammie stood watching Franco's rapid departure before she began to cry in earnest, her shoulders shaking violently. Selena's heart melted and she rushed to enfold her in her arms. "Hush. It will be all right."

"You'd better quit your crying, I know that." Trent's voice was ice-cold. Like steel. That made Pammie cry even harder.

"Trent, this is not the time nor place. You need to calm down."

He drew several deep breaths. "You're right. I'm just frustrated because I didn't expect this. I didn't expect to hear that my baby sister was making out with her boyfriend—" his right eye ticked at that word "—in the bathroom."

Pammie hiccuped and addressed her brother. "I d-don't like it wh-when you're m-mad at me." Her face was tear-streaked. "He took my phone."

Drawing her close, Selena said, "Oh, sweetheart. You know your brother loves you. It will be okay. And I'm sure he'll give you back your phone soon."

Trent rubbed his head and visibly tried to bring himself under control. "I'm not mad, I'm just…" He exhaled and dipped his chin to his chest. "I'm sorry for yelling. Let's go home. We'll talk later."

Pammie gave a nod and Selena suggested that

the young woman go wash her face. Once Pammie shuffled off to the restroom, Selena approached Trent and placed a hand on his arm. "How can I help you?" she asked instead of asking if he was okay. His distress was evident and he looked like he had a boulder on his back.

"I'm good." He bunched his fists. "I hate losing my temper with Pammie. I know better than that. It's just this is too much. Where did my innocent baby sister go? The one who liked the swings and the carousel."

"She's still there. She's just growing up."

"Mr. Greene told me to check out the transition home for Pammie. But how am I supposed to do that when I can't trust her to..." He shook his head.

"Can't trust her to what?" Selena pushed. "Remain a child?"

His shoulders slumped. "Yeah. I guess."

"Don't punish her for growing up. It's a problem to you, not to her. You can't fight against nature. And give her back her phone."

Pammie returned. Her reddened, puffy eyes pulled at Selena's heartstrings. She took each of their hands, bearing up the middle, and the trio made their way out of the building. The ride to Trent's place was filled with silence and Selena sat between them. She didn't try to engage either in conversation, choosing instead to let them feel and process. She was more than happy to assist if they needed it.

Then Selena's cell pinged. It was Nadine.

Girl. Don't kill me but I have to postpone our trip.

Selena grimaced. She silenced her notifications to keep it from sounding and then fired off her response.

Why? What happened?

Five nurses are out sick. Five. Some weird bug going around.

What? Wow. Okay. We can reschedule. Are you okay?

Yes. I think they got sick from the water fountain but you know I only drink bottled water.

Her eyes went wide before she giggled. Nadine was such a germaphobe and a conspiracist.

It's all good. Take care of yourself and reach out if you need anything.

We still on for Christmas though.

Selena sent a thumbs up, placed her cell phone in her bag and filled Trent in on her conversation with Nadine. She couldn't keep the disappointment of her voice. Though it had been Nadine's idea, Selena hadn't realized how much she had wanted to go until she wasn't going.

Trent's eyes brightened. "Well, I have a proposition that might put a smile on your face."

Her eyes narrowed. "What do you have in mind?"

He cleared his throat. "How about we meet up tomorrow to review the Valentine's Ball plans? And then you let me take you out on a date? A real date? A nice mix of business and pleasure."

"Why do you get to go on a date and I don't?" Pammie interjected, poking out her bottom lip. "That's not fair."

Trent scrunched his nose. "Because I'm grown—and watch your tone, young lady."

"Whatever. I'm grown, too." Pammie's lids fluttered as she executed a slow cut of the eyes before turning away from him to gaze out the window.

Trent's mouth dropped.

Selena bit back her smile. On the inside, she cheered for Pammie. The young woman was taking a stand. Asserting her independence. Trent must have decided not to engage Pammie in another argument, choosing instead to pull her phone out of his jacket and return it to his sister.

"Yes!" She pumped her fist. "I missed my phone."

Selena took that moment to put her contact information in Pammie's phone. "Call me if you need me."

Pammie nodded. "Okay." She tapped the screen. Within seconds, the sound of a cartoon on YouTube could be heard, though Pammie kept it low. Trent urged her to put in her AirPods and the young woman complied.

Selena felt the heat of Trent's gaze and made eye contact. He winked at her.

Her face grew hot. *Stop*, she mouthed, cocking her head toward Pammie.

He shrugged and blew her a kiss.

"You didn't answer me?" he whispered.

There had to be butterflies in her chest because her heart actually fluttered thanks to those brown eyes intently focused on her. Selena reached over to steeple her fingers with Trent's. "I'd love to," she said in a low tone. By this time, the cab swerved in front of Trent's building. Pammie hugged Selena before jumping out of the car. She didn't spare Trent a glance. Trent told the driver to keep the meter running.

"You've got a fight on your hands."

"It's nothing I can't handle." He sounded so sure that Selena didn't have to heart to tell him she doubted he was going to win a battle against Mother Nature.

Scooting close to Selena, he gave her a searing kiss before saying, "Dress super casual."

Her brows raised. "You're not taking me to a farm or camping, are you?" When he said no, her entire body relaxed. Thinking of the last time Trent had invited her somewhere, she made sure to ask, "Should I wear flats or sneakers?"

"Definitely sneakers. Nothing new or fancy."

Her nose wrinkled. She hadn't expected that answer. What kind of date did he have in mind? "Should I even bother to do my hair?" Her mouth dropped open when Trent appeared to give that question serious consideration. It was becoming obvious that his definition of a date and hers were vastly different.

"I'd say to wrap it in one of those head wrap thingies that you women like to wear and, whatever you do, do not wear your Sunday best."

Her mouth gaped. "Where on earth are you taking me and what time should I be ready?"

"About 2:00 p.m., and you'll see tomorrow." Trent patted her cheek. "I guarantee you'll be surprised."

Selena agreed because she already was surprised. It sounded like Trent wanted her to look haggard and unkempt for their date. He gave her another kiss before opening the door. "I've got to go see about Pammie, but I'll be thinking about you. Text you later."

As he jogged up the steps to Selena's place, holding two cans of specially mixed paint and a messenger bag across his torso, Trent second-guessed himself. Maybe he shouldn't have called his intentions for today a date, especially since it involved labor. But he had debated and debated on where to take Selena and what to do before he had asked her out. There was the usual fancy restaurants and chocolates and flowers, but Selena was used to that just from being a host on the show. He needed to be original. Give her an experience she would remember that had meaning. Impact.

Placing the cans on the stoop and ringing the doorbell, he knew for sure that today would be memorable. Whether or not she would understand and appreciate his intent was another matter. He could think of three words to sum up her potential reaction. Selena could either see him as sweet, corny, or cheap. He was counting on sweet.

She opened the door dressed in a large collegiate sweater, black jeans and a pair of black sneakers. Her hair had a scarf around it and she wore no makeup. She looked perfect for what he had planned.

Letting him inside, she ran her hands down her body. "Is this what you had in mind?"

Trent placed the cans by the door, draped his coat over them and raced after her to swoop her in his arms. She gasped in his ear, which made his body awaken. He gave her a tender kiss before placing her to stand and giving her the once-over. "You look beautiful."

She gave him the side-eye. "Really?"

"I'm seeing you. All of you in your natural state. And you're gorgeous."

Her lips pursed. "I'm also wearing granny panties. Will that make you swoon?" She placed a hand on her forehead for dramatic effect.

Trent cracked up. "Wouldn't matter to me one bit. I'm all about discovering what's underneath."

Her face reddened. She fiddled with her sweater. "How's Pammie doing?"

"She's good but upset that she's changing schools."

Selena appeared pensive. "Does she have to?"

"Yes. I don't want her near that boy." Even though thinking about his sister and Franco kissing in the bathroom made his blood boil, he'd pressed her for details. But Pammie had refused to tell him whose idea it was to meet in the girls' bathroom and she'd clammed up when he'd asked her about her top being open. If a teacher hadn't ventured into the restroom, who knew what else would have occurred.

"I don't think that's the right move. It's better if you have her acknowledge her feelings instead of suppressing them. Besides, what's to stop her from meeting another boy."

That was something he hadn't considered. Hmm… Maybe he would look into an all-girls school. He shoved his hands into his pockets. "I'm not going to have Pammie think what she did was cool."

Selena gave a light shrug. "Okay, I'm here if you need to talk about it. We can agree to disagree." She released a plume of air. "How about we get to work?"

He nodded; relieved she had decided to drop the subject. Trent hadn't slept well the night before, knowing Pammie was upset with him. She couldn't understand that Trent was only looking out for her. He had her best interests at heart. Always.

"Did you eat?"

She glared at him. "I had a light breakfast. Oatmeal. You don't plan to feed me on our date?"

"Yes, but I wasn't sure if you wanted us to nibble on something while we discuss the Valentine's Ball." He was making a muck of things. Trent flailed his arms. "Forget about it. Let's just get the menu and itinerary done for the dance."

They headed to the barstools and he dug into his messenger bag to retrieve two folders. Selena went to the refrigerator and took out two bottles of water and a small vegetable tray with Ranch dressing.

"When did you make this?"

"I didn't. I picked it up at the supermarket and transferred it to this platter. That was the extent of my labor." She placed the tray and bottles in front of them and took her a spot next to him before picking up one of the folders and flipping it open. He had a copy of their agreement and a small notepad in each folder.

Trent reached for a celery stick, dipped it in the dressing and plopped it into his mouth. He hadn't eaten breakfast, preparing for this date, so he was glad for something to tide him until dinner.

Selena looked through the pages before leaving to get her iPad.

"Let's look at the Gotham Hall website. I had one of the PR interns get in touch with the director of banquet service who's more than willing to meet with us, but I think it's a good idea if we scan the menu and have an idea of how we want to do this before we go in." With a few taps, she was on the venue's food and beverage webpage.

"I agree." He traced his finger along the bridge of his nose. "Do we want to offer refreshments?"

"Definitely."

"Great. We can have servers circulate with the food."

They scanned the appetizer and dessert selections, which were many. "Whoa. There are way more options than I thought."

Selena nodded and scratched her forehead. "Plus, we have to consider our vegetarian and vegan guests."

He released a sigh. "I'm overwhelmed already."

"Me, too…" She turned to him. "How about we meet with the director and schedule a taste test? That might help us decide. I don't know why I thought looking at the menu would be enough."

"We could leave this to the PR team considering the station is footing the bill," Trent suggested.

"Yes, but as you've pointed out, the producers really want us to provide the personal treatment. We want to be able to share our experiences with our listeners. It will generate a lot more excitement."

"Good point."

She closed the folder and reached for the legal pad. "Let's stay in our lane and plan the itinerary."

With a nod, Trent and Selena spent the next forty-five minutes sharing ideas of how to get the singles to interact. Speed dating? Mystery theater teams?

They jotted most down to review with Carla once they were back in the office. He released a whistle. "My brain hurts. This might be the one and only time we do this."

Selena giggled. "I doubt it. I predict this is going to be a hit, and a yearly thing. The first time is always the hardest. After this year, it will be a breeze."

Glancing at his watch, Trent packed up the papers and notes. "Now that work is finished, it's time to get to our time." He rubbed his hands together and then smiled.They had finished right on schedule.

She gave him a look of suspicion. "Where are we going looking like hobos?"

"We are staying right here." He jabbed a finger on the counter.

On cue, the doorbell rang.

Selena's eyes narrowed. "I wasn't expecting anything."

Trent splayed his hands. "I was. My delivery is here." He strutted to the door, like he owned the place, to let the two men inside. Selena hovered behind him. They walked in with paint rollers and brushes as well as a box of nails, tarp, plastic liner, a level and two hammers.

"What's going on?" Selena muttered, eyes blinking rapidly.

He kissed her cheek while his heart hammered. Now he knew he had probably made a mistake but there was no backstepping now. Trent signed off on the delivery and tipped the men before closing Selena's front door. He leaned back on the door and faced the woman whose eyes held fire.

"Care to tell me what this is all about?" She folded her arms, scanning the items, confusion evident.

He squared his shoulders. "We're putting some color on your walls. Add some zest to your place."

Her face went blank but he could see her chest heaving. "I see. And how is this a date?"

Trent swallowed. "Because we'll be doing it together."

Selena swung around and got her iPad. Then she stated, "According to the dictionary, a date is a social or romantic engagement. If I surveyed a hundred people, I'm almost positive ninety-nine percent would say painting my walls is a chore. So, tell me, how on earth is painting romantic?"

He had been prepared for this question. Trent puffed his chest and waggled his eyebrows. "Easy. None of those people has ever been painting with me."

Chapter Sixteen

Standing in her underwear—thank goodness she had worn a matching pair—covered with paint, her hair in shambles, pizza boxes scattered on the floor, Selena surveyed her coral-covered walls and fought back tears. For the first time since she had moved here, her place felt like a home.

She sniffled. "I like it." Then she twirled to face Trent, who sat in the center of the living room, his arms around his knees. "I like this a lot."

He grinned. "Somehow, I don't think you're just talking about your walls."

She ambled her way over to sit next to him and rested her head on his bare shoulder. "I'm not. Trent, you were so right. I can't think when last I had such a good time. Thank you."

He gave her a light jab. "I told you."

It was a wise move to cover the area with tarp because Trent had engaged her in a game of paint strip tag, which entailed tagging and splatting each other with paint. Of course, she had lost plenty of times, which is why her clothes were piled in a corner of the room and he was still in his jeans and undershirt. Both were covered with paint and she was pretty sure she had imbibed some with her pizza, but Selena felt content. The fact that they had contained the mess to the living area also helped her to keep her equilibrium.

"You brought me way out of my comfort zone today," she said. "This was great therapy for me."

"We're not done yet." He stood and wiped his palms on his jeans before holding out a hand. "You might have forgotten that I also purchased hammer and nails. These bare walls are beautiful but they are still sad."

She cocked her head. Was he talking about the walls or her? Nevertheless, she took his hand.

He tugged her to stand. "Where are those bins you told me about?"

Her stomach knotted. "I don't know if I can."

"You can. You should." His gentle voice soothed her warring insides. "But first, let's get cleaned up."

His words conjured up images of them both naked and wet, and her heart rate went into overdrive. "Um, I don't think that's a good idea."

"Get your mind out of fantasyland." Trent placed a hand over her lips. "I meant separate showers."

"I—I didn't…" she sputtered, knowing her cheeks were flushed. She raised her chin. "I know what you meant."

"Sure." Everything about his tone suggested Trent didn't believe her. He moved to unbuckle his belt and Selena saw that as her cue to give him some privacy.

She rolled her eyes and headed to her linen closet for spare towels. Her guest bathroom was well stocked to accommodate guests, though Nadine was the only person who actually stayed over.

Selecting a supersized towel, Selena placed it in the bathroom and returned to her living room in time to see a pair of firm butt cheeks outlined in dark blue boxer briefs pointed her way. Trent was bent over, rolling up the tarp along with his soiled clothes.

"Thanks for the show," she teased.

Trent almost fell over with surprise, but he spun to face her. "I didn't hear you coming."

"I assume you brought a spare set of clothes."

"Yes, I'm tossing these. That paint was oil-based. There's no getting that out."

She intended to do the same with her own. They paused for a beat, standing in their underwear, looking. Electric tingles zipped along her body as Trent scanned her from her feet upward, and she wasn't shy checking out his taut abs, muscled thighs and sculpted chest.

Then their eyes met.

Heat swelled within her. Selena coughed and gestured toward the bathroom. "Time to—"

"Get wet?" he interjected, moving close into her space.

"Uh…" Her chest heaved. Her mind conjured up memories of their tongues dueling in the back of the Town car. "I'll go first." Her eyes widened at her words.

"That's always my policy."

The promise in his voice was almost her undoing. "Quit flirting with me. You know what I meant. I meant I'm going to get showered." She released a deep breath and walked him to the guest bathroom. He used that chance to give her butt a light squeeze. They stopped outside the door.

He broke into a wide smile and opened the door. "I can't resist making your cheeks go all rosy." Trent gave her a playful pat. "Makes me wonder if the rest of you does the same."

Tossing her hair, she lifted her chin. "Today's not the day you'll find out."

"Fair enough." He shut the door in her face.

Selena could hear his chuckle as she stomped into her bedroom. They showered simultaneously and, as she lathered herself, she struggled with desire, thinking of the man who was also naked in the very next room, running his hands down that fit frame. It was erotic.

When she emerged from under the water, she hurriedly donned a sweat suit. Her wet tendrils hung loose on her shoulders and she shoved her feet into a pair of house slippers. She refused to look at her big, lonely bed and imagine how she could fill it in under thirty seconds if she just uttered the words. She was just getting to know Trent on a personal level and though the chemistry was evident—boy, was it—she couldn't let it interfere with what was best. Selena was determined to do what she would advise her own clients, if she still had any. And that was to take it slow.

Never mind that under the drab clothes, she had chosen a set of lacy gray-and-pink bra and panties to wear underneath. A *Something's Gotta Give* gift from Nadine. A just-in-case move. Taking it slow might evolve to mean taking her clothes off slow, building the heat slow, grinding him slow. She exhaled.

Think of something else, Selena. You sound sex-starved.

I am.

She found Trent in the kitchen, finishing a cold slice of pizza. It was pretty dark outside. Eyeing the clock, she was shocked to see it was close to 7:00 p.m. Trent gave her a sexy smile. "Here you are. Did everything come off okay?"

"Yes. I used the rubbing alcohol first, like you instructed. I see you're good, too."

He was dressed in slim-fit jeans, a checkered shirt and coordinated sneakers. Selena could smell his cologne from across the room. Her stomach tightened, imagining that scent fused with hers, tangled in her sheets.

Another exhale. Goodness. She needed a drink of water.

"Let's do this," Trent said, standing and stretching, giving her a view of his taut abdomen.

Selena picked her way to her bedroom closet and opened the door. She stood, frozen, eyeing the bins. Trent came up behind her and drew her into him. She snuggled into him. "I've got a lot of memories in those bins."

"We'll tackle it one at a time. How does that sound?"

Selena nodded. Trent lifted one and they returned to the living room area to settle on her couch. She lifted the lid while Trent went to retrieve a hammer. The first thing she saw was her high school graduation photo. The next was a family picture of Selena with her parents during their happy times. When they'd been a family. When her only concern had been what was for dinner. She held the picture close to her chest. Surprise tears wet her cheeks. She wiped her eyes with the back of her index finger.

"We can put it away, if you want, so you don't have to look at it."

She straightened. For many years she had done that. Hide. Maybe it was time to cease. "No. It's my history. I didn't fall out of the sky. I had a mother and a father." Holding the frame high, she said, "Put it up."

With a nod, Trent took out the level and got to

work. Ten minutes later, her first family picture graced her wall. Standing back and peering at the grinning faces, she smiled. "I like it."

Selena stormed over to the bin with gusto and grabbed other relics from her past. With Trent's assistance and prodding, she brandished her numerous awards, trophies and diplomas through her house. Relics from some of her travels also went on display and, when she was finished, she wrapped her arms about her and drew in a satisfied breath. She finally felt at home.

Trent came to her side and tugged her close. She leaned her head on his shoulder, enjoying the feel of his hand on her back. It grounded her. "Thank you, Trent. I will never forget today."

"Like I said. I wanted you to have a date to remember. For life."

All she could do was nod. Selena knew she was going to circulate her house a few times and take it all in. "Should I order takeout?" she asked, seeing it was now close to 9:00 p.m.

"Nah. I'd better get home." Trent yawned. "I'm taking Pammie to Florida for a couple of days. We're going to hit up all the theme parks and soak in some sun."

Disappointment made her shoulders droop but she was determined to appear unaffected. "Have enough fun for me, as well." Great. Now she sounded pitiful and like she was angling for an invite.

"You're welcome to come with us," he said.

"No. I'm going to enjoy my home for a few days. Spend some time treasuring my space." She walked him to the door and they shared a heated, passionate kiss. One that made her toes curl.

He wore a satisfied grin. The man knew what he was doing to her. He blew her a kiss. "I look forward to sexting you."

"Sexting?"

"Yeah. I need something to get me through the lonely nights ahead. Besides, I'm a master at words. As you will soon see."

"Looking forward to it." She closed the door behind him and leaned against it. Then she sighed. She missed his presence already. The house didn't feel as full without him in it. Selena shook off the doldrums. "Snap out of it, girl. You've done without Trent for years. A few days is no big whoop. You'll be quite all right."

Trent was not all right. Right before they were supposed to leave, Pammie had declared she didn't want to go to Disney World. Said it was for babies. Said her friends were having a sleepover and she wanted to go to that instead.

"Which friends?" he'd asked.

"My best friends, Rosa and Emily, from school," she'd said.

"We're going to Orlando," he'd said.

"I'm not going anywhere," were her last words.

Then she'd sat on the couch and refused to move.

Trent stood on his balcony, fuming and replaying their conversation in his mind. He had already reached out to Dontae and James who were on their way over to talk to Pammie.

He briefly considered reaching out to Selena, because she was in fact a therapist and the ideal person to provide assistance. But Trent didn't feel like hearing that Pammie was growing up and how he needed to change.

He exhaled; his breath puffy in the brisk cold, and wondered who had body snatched his easygoing, docile sister and replaced her with this impertinent, pouty individual. The shell was his sister but she wasn't the same person on the inside. She was different. She was…

A grown woman?

He gripped the railing. *No. No. No.*

"Hey, man, Pammie is mad at you," Dontae said, walking up to him. Trent had placed his friends on the open visitors list so they could enter his penthouse from the private elevator.

"I know. We were supposed to be 30,000 feet in the air but she's adamant that she's not going to Florida with me."

Dontae's eyes narrowed. "Why?"

"She wants to spend the night at a friend's house."

His friend placed a hand on his hip. "And what's wrong with that?"

"I don't allow that."

"She has to socialize with people her own age."

"That's what school is for. She gets all the so-cialization she needs under the watchful eye of a teacher."

Dontae shook his head. "Are you listening to your-self? You're acting like you're a puppeteer. You can't keep Pammie on a string. She has to find her own way. Bruh, it's time for you to relinquish control."

He clenched his jaw. "You jumping on that band-wagon? You know I can't let anything happen to her." His voice cracked.

Dontae patted his arm. "I get it, bruh. But, it's time. It's time."

Their conversation was cut short once James strolled outside, holding a bottled water in one hand and a sandwich in the other. "Pammie asked me to talk to you and see if you'll change your mind." James chomped into his sandwich.

"Really?" Dontae asked. "Only you would stop to help yourself to something to eat when our friend is having a crisis."

"What? I gotta eat so I have my strength in case I need to give somebody a beatdown." James shrugged his massive shoulders.

Trent tuned out his friends' bickering. His mind was too full of his sister to focus on anything else. "I can't believe Pammie isn't backing down," he mut-tered.

"She's twenty-one years old, Trent. If you ask me, her behavior is normal."

Trent bunched his fists. "If someone tells me one

more time what's normal, I'm going to…" He released a bellow of frustration. "Why can't anyone get that I can't lose her?"

James's brow creased. "How are you losing her?"

"She's not trying to leave the planet, Trent," Dontae chimed in. "She wants to hang with girls her age and put on makeup and talk about boys or whatever they do at that age."

"Speaking of boys…" Trent gave his friends a quick rundown of what had happened with Pammie and Franco.

To his surprise, James bowled over laughing. "Bruh, if you see your face. I can't believe the guy who asked twin sisters out to watch two different movies when he was twenty is behaving like a prude."

"Oh, snap. I had forgotten that." Dontae snickered. "Then when the girls found out, he tried to act like he didn't know they were sisters."

Trent spoke through his teeth. "This is different." He loved having longtime friends who knew his history but hated it at the same time.

Dontae sobered first. "I said a few minutes ago that it's time. It's time that you accept you couldn't control your parents' death. You didn't make them try to drive back from North Carolina in a snowstorm."

"No, but I was the one who paid for that vacation weekend to the Outer Banks."

James rested a hand on his shoulder. "There's a

reason it was called an accident, Trent. It means no one was at fault. It's time to forgive yourself, bruh."

Trent lowered his head. "I'm all she has left and she's my only living relative. Because of me, Pammie lost our parents. I can't allow anything to happen to her."

"She has to live her own life, though. She has to make mistakes," James said. "You taught her well and, what you didn't know, you provided through the best schools and resources. All these years, you taught us by your example not to focus on her disability but on her capabilities."

"She'll never truly be fully independent," Trent said.

"Yes, but that doesn't mean that she has to remain completely dependent on you for the rest of her life," Dontae added.

Those words punctured his gut.

"Maybe instead of resisting, you can help Pammie. If you're scared, imagine how she must feel."

Trent's softly spoken words penetrated his stubborn resolve and he acknowledged the truth. Trent's shoulders slumped. "You're both so right. I have been holding her back. Selena's been trying to tell me this but I refused to listen. I feel like the world's biggest jerk."

Dontae chucked him on the shoulder. "I think you're way too hard on yourself. You are not the biggest jerk in the world. Maybe you're the biggest jerk in NYC, but definitely not across the globe."

Trent chuckled. Trust these guys to keep him humble. "Thank you for that." He hugged his friends and went to seek out his sister to talk.

This time, he didn't lecture. He listened. He found out three things. Pammie wanted to get a job. She wanted to learn how to drive. And she wanted to get her own place. All adult things. Things he promised her he would help her do.

Trent swallowed his fears and told Pammie to invite her friends and their parents over after Christmas so he could meet them. It was a start. If he liked the parents, he would consider the sleepover.

For a brief second, Trent thought about purchasing them all tickets to Disney, but common sense prevailed and he decided to host a small New Year's Eve dinner instead since Pammie's friends and families had most likely made plans to bring in the new year, Trent would host it early enough so they could eat and then go party elsewhere. The more he thought about it, the more he liked the idea.

And he knew exactly who to ask to be his plus-one.

Chapter Seventeen

It was as if someone had put a microphone by her heart. That's how loud the sound of her heartbeat resonated in her ear. Her chest heaved and her palms were sweaty as she stood in the elevator minutes before 7:00 p.m. heading up to Trent's penthouse suite. All this nervousness because Trent had asked her to be his plus-one.

Like his *date* date. A fancy dress, hair in an updo, foundation-on-the-face kind of date.

Selena had accepted since it was a private get-together at his house that didn't include anyone in their work circle. Then she had dashed to Nordstrom and left thirty minutes later with a black Mac Duggal long-sleeved, embellished cocktail dress. Selena loved the feel of the beadwork, the velvet flowers and fit of the flared mesh skirt. It even had velvet on the hem. She had paired it with a Sam Edelman classic stiletto.

For a brief second, before the elevator doors whooshed open, Selena wondered if she had over-dressed, but then shrugged. It was too late to go home, so she exited with a confident smile.

She scanned the room glittered with the typical New Year's decorations. There were three other cou-ples milling about the space, along with James and Dontae. Trent had some old school music playing and she bopped her head to the beat. And it smelled like some good old-fashioned home cooking. Her mouth watered and her stomach complained. She hoped Trent had used the same people who'd catered his dinner at the shelter.

When Trent spotted her, his eyes brightened and those lips expanded into a wide smile. Selena preened. She had obviously understood the assign-ment. Trent wore a slim-fitted suit, she would guess Giorgio Armani, and a white dress shirt. The man was delicious-fine.

Pammie and two other young women were hud-dled together, dancing to the music under Min-dy's watchful eye. Selena waved at Pammie, who screeched when she saw Selena. Pammie and her friends dashed over to greet her. All three had donned cocktail dresses and each wore a pair of kitten heels. Pammie wore a side-ruched, formfitting blue dress. One of her friends was wearing a pink number with an asymmetrical hem and the other had on a green dress, snug at the top with rows of mini-tulle on the bottom.

"Ms. Selena!" Pammie held out her arms and Selena hugged her tight.

"You guys look fabulous," Selena said. From the corner of her eye, she could see Trent coming toward her, but he got waylaid by James and Dontae.

The girls giggled.

"Trent took us shopping and bought us dresses." Each girl struck a pose.

"Yeah, and he paid for us to get our hair done," the one in green said, patting her curls.

Selena nodded. "That is wonderful." She made eye contact with Pammie. "What are your friends' names?"

"This is Rosa," Pammie said, pointing to the one in pink. "And that's Emily." She pointed to the other in green.

"It's great to meet you Rosa and Emily."

"Nice to meet you," each said.

Pammie beamed. "Rosa has her driver's license and Emily has a job."

"I work at a school," Emily said. "I work from 3:00 p.m. to 6:00 p.m. every Monday to Friday. I love helping with the little children."

Selena placed a hand over her chest. "I'm sure the children love having you, as well."

"Trent says he's going to help me get a job, too,"

Pammie said. "Then we can all live together one day." The girls held hands, jumped and squealed.

Selena's heart expanded at their joy. It was infectious. "Do you know what you want to do?" she asked Pammie, though she didn't expect an answer.

Pammie's response was swift, like she had been mulling on it for a while. "I've thought and thought about it, and I think I want to be a greeter. I think I would be good at it. My teacher says I am friendly and I have a great personality."

Selena nodded. "I agree." She held in her surprise. Selena just knew Pammie would've said that she wanted to sing, but she had chosen something stable that would give her good income. Smart girl.

Rosa tossed her hair. "I want to be a model like Sofía Jirau."

Selena wrinkled her nose. "Sofia who?"

"She's a Victoria's Secret model and she has Down's syndrome like me."

"Wow. I didn't know that," Selena said. "I didn't know what I wanted to do when I was your age, so I'm impressed with each of you."

"Let's go get something to drink," Rosa said, dragging Pammie by the arm. Emily followed.

Selena bit back a smile at their speedy departure, but her heart was full. Something must have happened for Trent to have changed his position. When he'd called to invite her, he had told her that he would explain in person. She was eager to hear what he had to say.

He was now talking with a couple of other parents. She decided to obey her stomach's call and traipse over to the buffet area. Trent had hired two servers.

Trent came over and the other guests used that as a sign to form a queue.

Grabbing a dinner plate, Selena handed one to Trent. He thanked her by giving her a forehead kiss, causing her to shiver on the inside. She passed on the seafood and selected stewed chicken, potato salad, string beans and some steamed corn. He selected the same, except he had added tilapia and collard greens. He also made sure to make some sort of physical contact, grazing her arm, blowing in her ear, that made Selena center on him. The man. And on maintaining a grip on her plate.

"Where are you going to put all that?" she asked once they were seated at the large dinner table. There were tall glasses of iced tea and she took a sip. This was the first time she would be eating that day and her stomach was about to be real happy.

"I have to keep up my energy," he said with a wink. "Something I hope you'll experience the benefits of very soon."

Selena almost spewed the contents of her tea. "Would you behave, please?" She looked around to see if they had attracted attention, but everyone was focused on their food. Then she asked Trent to explain the reason behind his spontaneous house party. When he told her about Pammie's stance, Selena silently cheered.

At that moment, another visitor arrived. Selena's mouth dropped. "Nadine's here. I didn't know she was coming." Her best friend wore a dark red cocktail dress and strappy gold shoes. Like Selena, she must have hung her coat by the rack near the elevator.

"Yeah. James invited her."

She wrinkled her nose. "Where's Dontae? I thought I saw him earlier."

"He had to work, so he grabbed a plate to go."

"Oh, I see." Selena chuckled because she would have done the same thing.

Trent dug into his meal, dipping his fork into the tilapia. He dangled it near her mouth. "You want a taste?"

She could smell the thinly sliced Scotch bonnet. "I'll try a little." Her mouth closed over the fork and she slid the food into her mouth.

Trent's eyes darkened. His lips quirked. "Can you do that again?"

She chuckled and gave him a shove. "You're a trip. I can't with you."

"You're a desirable woman."

Nadine and James came to sit by them. "Are we interrupting?" Nadine asked, her grin mischievous.

"Please tell me we are," James added.

"You're more than welcome." Selena waved a hand. "We're just kicking it. Having fun."

Nadine rolled her eyes. "You guys can tell yourselves that all you want. You're not seeing what we're seeing. Chem-is-try."

Trent had a quick comeback. "We need chemistry if we want to work together on the air."

"And off the air," James said.

Shifting in her seat, Selena concentrated on her plate. "Sometimes we see what we want to see, even if it isn't the truth." This thing between her and Trent was too new to talk about or dig deep. Neither of them was ready to have that discussion.

Of course, James had another comment. "And sometimes we don't see the truth because we're one of those people who insists on wearing shades even when the sun ain't shining."

"Will you quit it?" Trent glared at his friend until James lifted a hand and backed down.

Selena caught how Nadine naturally snuggled in his arms. "What we need to talk about is you two. What's going on there?"

James focused on his plate. "We good. We're just enjoying each other's company."

Nadine stuffed her mouth with food.

"Don't think I didn't see your Twix moment," Selena teased, referring to the commercial where people avoided difficult conversations by chewing on a Twix. From the first time they'd seen the commercial, when the friends didn't want to talk about something, they called it a Twix moment. Nadine pursed her lips and shrugged.

Fortunately, Pammie and her friends came over. The girls' conversations and antics served as a great distraction. The rest of the evening, Trent and Selena made an effort to get to know the girls' parents before they left. She could see Trent liked them and prayed that Trent would keep his word and help his sister achieve her personal goals. Pammie had escaped to her room leaving Trent, Selena, James and Nadine to rehash the night's success.

Her Apple Watch vibrated and she saw a familiar number on the screen. Selena dug into her purse and answered her cell phone, walking into one of the guest rooms. Her heart thumped against her chest as she waited to hear the reason for the call.

"Ms. Cartwright? I'm calling about your mother." The man on the line identified himself as the director of the Gracie Square Hospital.

"What's wrong? Is she all right?" Selena asked.

Trent followed her inside and she placed the call on speaker.

"Your mother is going to be placed on a 72-hour health watch."

Her knees buckled and she dropped onto the bed. "Wh-what?"

"Your mother wrote a note about wanting to end her life. It was after a difficult session where she came to realization that her husband had died. She hasn't spoken since, so we're transferring her to another floor with a personal caretaker."

"Oh, no." Selena struggled to catch her breath, feeling like she had been punched in the stomach. Trent's hand snaked around her shoulders and he gave her a squeeze. She leaned into him and told the director, "I'm coming to see her." Her fingers shook and she cupped the phone with two hands.

"Visiting hours have passed. You can see her to-morrow."

"No. I will see my mother now."

"Ms. Cart—"

Trent took the phone. "We are on our way over there and when we get there, you'll grant Selena ten minutes. Ten minutes so Selena can see that her mother is okay."

The man on the line released a breath. "Fine. I'll see what I can do. But no more than ten minutes."

Selena was inconsolable. She spent the entire cab ride sobbing into his chest as she berated herself for abandoning her mother. The more Trent repeated that it wasn't her fault, the more she cried.

He knew it was because she was scared, but her mother was the one who had pushed Selena away. He was so glad that he had listened to his instincts and followed her into the guest room. Although, when he'd seen her stroll in there, he'd had a different impression, thinking she wanted to have a private make-out session before leaving.

"Yeah, but she's not well, and I know that. I should have still visited."

"She kicked you out," Trent said. "Basically, blamed you for her relationship's demise. Don't go painting her as a saint because she's ill."

Selena clutched his coat. "Regardless, I can't lose her. She's all I have left."

"Nonsense," he shot back. "You have me." Trent stiffened. He had tossed out the words in an effort to comfort her, but he was surprised at the realization that he meant them. He wanted—no, needed—to be there for Selena. Snatching her close and kissing the top of her head, he repeated, "You have me."

She sniffled and shuddered against him before closing her eyes. She puckered her lips to keep the sobs inside. Tears trekked down her face, causing Trent's heart to constrict. Based on what she'd told him, Selena's mother didn't deserve those tears. They rolled down her chin nonstop and Trent wiped them with his hand before he remembered he had some napkins in his coat. Retrieving them, Trent gently dabbed her face as he soothed her.

"Your mother is still here and, while she's still breathing, there's a chance."

Selena lifted her head, her eyes filled with hope, like his words had been a lifeline. Trent prayed that Helen would be all Selena needed her to be. And if not, like he said, he wasn't going anywhere. He patted her back and encouraged her to rest. Now that Selena was somewhat calmer, Trent sent James a text to let him know why he had left and to ask him to let Nadine know. He was sure both James and Nadine had missed his presence. Unless, of course, they had wandered off to sneak in some couple time. Trent certainly had enough space for entertaining.

James's response was quick.

You need us to come down there?

No. They aren't allowing visitors.

Got it. Keep us posted.

Will do.

He slipped his phone in his pocket as the cab pulled to the curb. Selena sprang up and straightened. After directing the driver to wait, he told Selena, "Go on. I'll be here waiting." She had the door open before the driver put the gear in Park. He watched her scuttle inside, the wind whipping at her hair, before leaning back in the leather seat. Then he called Mindy to let her know he had left with Selena.

Fifteen minutes later, he saw the door open and Selena rushing outside. Moving off pure emotion, Trent jumped out and held open his arms.

She plopped against him and wrapped her arms around him. He ran his finger through her wind-tossed curls and cupped her face before giving her a tender kiss. Holding hands, they dived into the cab.

Trent rubbed his hands. "It's brick cold out there. How did the visit go?"

"She was sedated, but when she saw me, she gave me a smile. Most of the time she rambled on, but at least she didn't yell at me to leave."

Her little shrug pierced his heart. No one should be uncertain of a parent's love. Trent told the driver to take them back to his place. He tensed, hoping Selena wouldn't object, but she gave a shy nod. Trent deduced she didn't want to be alone, which was good, because he wouldn't have been able to sleep well knowing she was in turmoil.

"Will you be able to see her tomorrow?" he asked.

Selena nodded. "It will be another short visit but they plan to keep her under suicide-watch for at least the ten days while they complete their evaluation." She rested her head against his. "Thank you for coming. Knowing you were here, waiting, gave me strength to see my mother."

"I'm glad I could be here for you."

She cupped his face with her hands. "You're not the man I thought you were, Trent Moon. You're better and so much more." Her eyes filled.

Her words warmed him to his core. He touched her chin. "No more tears tonight. Okay?"

"Okay." She gave a tentative smile.

Trent took in her reddened eyes, nose and blotchy cheeks, and his heart tripped. Unbelievable. Slightly panicked, he explained the phenomenon by telling himself that it was a natural reaction to an emotional night. To keep from voicing a sentiment he didn't mean, Trent dipped his head and crushed his lips to hers.

Chapter Eighteen

They kissed in the back of the cab, inside the elevator, until they entered Trent's penthouse, and Selena was there for it. Whew. This man knew how to use his lips, his tongue, and Selena was pretty sure she had never been kissed like this in her entire life. Her body was on fire. Her mind was mush. Her tongue parched. Her thoughts centered on one person: Trent.

He tossed their coats somewhere. She curved into his body and gasped when Trent lifted her into his arms. Then he carried her to his large bedroom. Somewhere along the way, she dropped her purse but was too enthralled to care. The sensor made his lights come on, though they were dimmed. Her mouth dropped.

Trent excused himself to use his private bathroom

and to check on Pammie, telling Selena to get comfortable.

Slowly, she stood and took in Trent's private space. The skyline was incredible and ceiling-to-floor windows gave a magnificent view of the city at night. The gray wall with beautiful one-of-a-kind art pieces, the round couch with blue pillows, a small rock fountain and *that* bed. That bed, with its luxurious-looking covers, that required two steps made of marble to get to. A California king with a custom upholstered-panel headboard mounted on the wall set against another breathtaking scene and a private patio. Goodness. If she were Trent, she would never leave this…this oasis.

Light music flowed through the space, indicating that Trent had wired his surround sound into the walls. This room was epitome of seduction. Selena was inexperienced and…unsure if the expectation was that she would be undressed and waiting for him to join her in bed. So she stood there, rooted in the same spot where he had left her. Waiting.

Trent returned with two glasses of water. He had ditched his suit jacket and shoes, and pulled his shirt out of his pants. He led her to the couch and snuggled next to her.

"Thank you." She lowered her eyes and took a sip. From where she sat, she had a direct view of the bed.

He pinned her with a gaze. "We don't have to do this, you know."

She rounded on him. "We are doing this."

He chuckled. "Okay, if you insist. I'll gladly oblige. It's just…when I returned, you looked frozen like a scared rabbit."

"I'm not running anywhere." Her heart pounded and her hands shook, but it was from anticipation and not fright. "I plan to start the new year off with a bang." And an orgasm.

Taking the glass out of her hand, Trent rested both drinks on the glass nightstand, stood and held out a hand. When she placed her hand in his, he pulled her flush against him. "Dance with me." He gyrated his hips into hers and, after releasing a shaky breath, Selena matched his every move. While they danced, he unzipped her dress and she allowed it to shimmer down her body and to fall into a puddle at her feet. She undid his buttons and slipped off his shirt, greedy to get her hands on his chest. It was smooth to the touch. She leaned into him, inhaling his scent, and smiled. His hands explored her body, reigniting the spark and making her ache for more than a touch.

She moaned.

Trent hoisted her in his arms and placed her on his bed before slipping off her shoes and sheer tights. His eyes scanned her fiery red lingerie with a possessiveness that scorched her skin. She lifted her arms.

"I'm coming, baby." Trent shed the rest of his clothes and stood before her. Selena gulped. His reputation hadn't done him justice. That was her last thought before Trent kissed her, arousing her passions to a dangerous height, making her sweat, making her scream—once he assured her the room was soundproof—and leading Selena to the very first *Something's Gotta Give* moment of her life. Bliss. Finally, sweet bliss.

He had a woman in his bed. His private domain. A good start to the new year. That was Trent's first thought when the sun's bright beams filled his bedroom. Selena lay sprawled against him, her curls splayed across the pillow, and she was tucked under his arm. He reached for the remote on the side of his bed and pressed a button to close the blind and darken the space.

Slipping from under the blanket, Trent dressed in a pair of flannel pajamas, took care of his morning routines and wandered into the kitchen. Pammie was already there, eating cereal with an apple and banana by her bowl. Bits of cereal were scattered on the countertop.

"Ms. Mindy left to go see her mom," Pammie said after greeting him. "I didn't see you, so I made myself something to eat." She was dressed in loungewear and appeared to have already showered. She had gotten her hair cornrowed in preparation for their Disney trip, so her hair was good to go.

Trent kissed his sister on the cheek and went to retrieve eggs and pancake mix. It was Mindy's day off and he usually prepared pancakes or waffles for himself and Pammie. He put a fry pan on the burner and turned the stove on medium heat.

"Are you making pancakes?" she asked.

"Yes, do you want some? Oh, and happy New Year."

"Happy New Year." She grinned. "I tried to stay up but I fell asleep before the ball dropped."

"You can watch the recording later."

He poured the mix into a bowl and added water. Once he had mixed the batter, Trent placed it on the counter and brewed a cup of coffee in the Keurig. If he knew Selena, she would be wanting this as soon as she was up.

She pointed to the bowl. "Can I help? I want to learn how to cook."

Visions of his sister burning herself made his stomach tense. "I'm only making a small batch this time. But I tell you what, I'll hire someone to teach you. How's that?"

Pammie nodded and Trent relaxed. She kept up a steady stream of conversation, talking about the party yesterday, her friends, and what she wanted to do at a sleepover. Just as Trent finished prepping the eggs, Selena walked out wearing one of his T-shirts and drawstring shorts. She had them pulled tight at the waist, like Steve Urkel tight, to keep the shorts from falling to the floor.

As soon as Pammie saw her, her mouth dropped. "Ms. Selena, you're here. I didn't even know you were here." Pammie scooted off the barstool and almost jumped into Selena's arms.

"Good morning, Pammie. You look wonderful."

Trent bit back a smile. Selena was trying to change the subject.

"When did you get here?"

Selena's eyes shot to his, panicked. They hadn't discussed the morning after. Though he had never had a woman stay over before Selena, Trent shrugged. As Selena and Pammie kept pointing out, she was grown.

He rescued Selena from responding by saying, "Ms. Selena spent the night after the party."

Selena's walked over to greet him with a light punch on the arm. Trent chuckled. He realized she was being discreet because Pammie was present and watching them with intense curiosity.

Selena sniffed. "Everything smells delicious." Looking down at her bare feet, she covered her mouth and whispered, "I'm not sure if you have a spare toothbrush I could use?"

"Sure. You can find everything you need in any one of the guest rooms." Eyeing her curls, he offered, "I even have hair products you could use."

"Wow. You're prepared."

Trent raised a brow. "That's just how I am." Once the words left his mouth, Trent froze. Maybe Pammie wouldn't pick up on the fact that Selena had slept in his room.

Selena's face flushed and she shuffled out of the kitchen after saying she was going to brush her teeth.

Pammie cocked her head. "Trent, did Selena sleep over in your room?"

He wasn't about to lie to his sister, so Trent nodded. "Yep."

"Oh." Pammie fell silent.

He watched her mind process what he had revealed and busied himself by placing their food on the table along with the coffee and some fruit. By the time he was finished, Selena re-entered the room.

"Ms. Selena, why are you wearing Trent's clothes?" Pammie asked.

Selena coughed and tucked her chin to her chest. "I didn't want to mess up my dress and so Trent loaned me something to wear."

"Oh."

Her wrinkled brow meant her mind continued to churn. Trent knew the dam of questions would soon be released.

Pammie walked over and pulled out a chair to join them. Seeing that she hadn't eaten her fruit, Trent gave her half of a pancake and poured a generous amount of syrup. He doubted Pammie would be able to eat more than that.

"Is she your girlfriend?" his sister asked, syrup running down her chin. He stiffened. He wasn't prepared to answer that question.

Trent grabbed a napkin from the center of the table and moved to wipe her face, but Pammie tilted her head from him. "I can do it." She cleaned her face before asking the same question again.

"We're really good friends," Selena picked at her food, gesturing to him to provide confirmation.

Trent's answer was more direct. "Yes, we're dating." He thought he heard Selena exhale but he couldn't be certain. Maybe she had been unsure of his position.

Pamela's mouth rounded. "Oh."

That third *Oh* concerned him. His sister still wasn't satisfied. However, since he was ravenous, Trent devoured his meal. His night with Selena had caused him to use even his reserve energy. She had been his equal in the sheets, and in stamina. Trent was already looking forward to more nights in her arms.

"Does this mean you're in love with each other?" Pammie asked, her last slice of pancake dangling on her fork. "And are you getting married? Because I want to be in the wedding." She perked up. "Can Rosa and Emily be in the wedding, too?"

Sweat beads lined his forehead. His sister was moving faster than he had expected. "That's not how it works, sis."

"But you've never had anybody spend the night before." Her eyes were clouded with confusion.

Trent heard Selena's intake of breath but he was determined she wouldn't think that meant more than it did. "Yes, that's true. But Ms. Selena is a really good friend. We're having fun. That's all." He spoke with a tone of finality, hoping his sister understood, because this topic was making him squirm on the inside.

Selena chimed in. "Yes, we're nowhere close to

being in love. We're just having a good time. Nothing serious." Hearing the certainty in her tone made uncertainty rise within him.

"Okay, I guess." Pammie finally let the subject go, declaring she was going to work on her TikTok videos.

Trent ducked his head so Selena wouldn't see that her carefree words had left him sucker-punched. He knew she'd been trying to temper Pammie's enthusiasm but he didn't get how she could be so blasé about a sexual experience that had been nothing short of amazing.

She had rocked his world, causing him to lose control. But he couldn't say all that to his sister, so he had downplayed it. Trent hadn't expected Selena to agree so easily.

To her, it appeared as if it was just another day, another dude, between the sheets. That rankled. He didn't like feeling like he was a pair of shoes Selena could buy or return to the rack, forgotten. Especially since he was craving more. Way more. Not love, but a step above fun, whatever that was. Like a blend of fun and a huge dollop of respect and laughter and passion. But it was evident Selena wasn't on the same wavelength and he had been mistaken.

He wouldn't make that mistake again.

Chapter Nineteen

Something was off with her and Trent. The vibe between them had cooled considerably after breakfast. Trent had appeared sulky but when she'd asked, his response had been, "I'm good." A sure sign that he wasn't.

That was why Selena had changed back into her dress and was now in the elevator and heading for home. Before leaving, she had called to check on her mother's welfare, relieved to learn that Helen had eaten and taken a shower. Great signs. When she'd informed Trent, his response had been somewhat subdued. He had held her hand and insisted on walking her out, but his manner was polite, his tone cool. And he hadn't asked her to stay.

That cut at her heart. Maybe he had been disappointed in her performance. *No.* That wasn't it. Maybe he had enjoyed himself too much and that scared him. Actually, the more she thought about it, his attitude had changed after Pammie had asked about them being in love. He had been quick to let his sister know it was all about fun. Just fun.

And she had quickly agreed. Even though her night with Trent had been epic and she had felt a close connection, a bond that she had never had with another man, she couldn't let Trent think she wanted more than they'd agreed upon. Because she didn't.

Why would she want anything of substance with a renowned ladies' man? He had given all that he could offer, was upfront about it, so she shouldn't be all in her feelings. But she was.

Because he wasn't who she'd thought he was and yet, last night, he was everything she'd needed him to be. Generous, hot, nasty all rolled up in tall, smooth, dark packaging. She panted, remembering how she had felt secure, treasured and desired. How her toes had curled as her body climaxed time and time again.

Whew.

She'd had more than fun. She'd had an experience. And she wanted him all to herself, at least for a little bit. Selena hated the thought of those lips and hands on anyone who wasn't her.

She gasped.

Jealousy and possessiveness did not equate to fun. She forgave herself the emotions because the man had given her *The Big O.* She wasn't the cold fish the handful of men had accused her of being. For a second, she debated texting her exes her happy news. But a minute of petty could have lifetime consequences, so she refrained.

However, she knew just who she could tell. Selena wasn't a sex-and-blab kind of girl but she couldn't keep this to herself. With a squeal, she pulled out her phone and texted Nadine.

Something got given girl and I took it all and then some.

It took a moment for Nadine to text back.

I'm screaming. Woot. Woot. You're finally a woman now.

Selena rolled her eyes and cracked up.

Whatever.

Let's get together and celebrate.

And they did. Later that night, Selena and Nadine met up at their favorite karaoke bar after Selena closed on the house. She deposited her check and was ready to celebrate. The friends challenged themselves to sing songs about sex: "Sexual Healing," "Let's Talk About Sex," "I'll Make Love To You." The list went on until someone in the crowd pleaded for them to stop. On a whim, because she missed him, kind of, and she wanted to see if he was still in a funk, Selena sent Trent a clip of Ginuwine's song "Pony."

He responded with "Rock the Boat."

When she saw that, Selena hugged her friend goodbye and had her fast tail back at Trent's place in under a half hour, where they'd brought those songs to life under his sheets.

That was why, once again, Selena had found herself leaving Trent's house way past midnight. They had an early morning meeting with Carla to go over the order for their expanded show.

A meeting she was ten minutes late getting to because she'd had to fix the dark circles under her eyes thanks to her messing around with Trent. Meanwhile, he looked refreshed with his wide smile and those beautiful teeth. And he smelled so good. So good. *Ugh.* What was she doing ogling his butt and the outline in the front of his jeans like she was lovesick puppy? They were at work and they had agreed, at Selena's insistence, to keep this relation *thing* between them. Their *bene*friendship.

Carla gave her a firm look. "You're late."

"Got caught in traffic," she fibbed.

Trent gave her a cup of coffee and sat across from her. "Just the way you like it."

Her insides tingled at those seemingly innocent words. Words he had used that very morning right before she'd had an earthshaking, foot-stomping, lift-your-hand-and-shout-hallelujah release. She muttered a quick thanks. The man had the nerve to grin and puff his chest. He knew what he was doing to her.

She would ignore him. Or try to anyway. But later… Later would be payback. She bit back a smile. Oh, was she looking forward to that.

Donning her cloak of professionalism, Selena read one of the two letters she would address that day. Her tongue went dry and her ardor cooled. "Um, Carla, can we have the assistants choose a different topic?"

Carla frowned. "But office romance is juicy and messy. And this man is heartbroken and he has to see this woman's face every day. You can give him advice and then offer him a ticket to the Valentine's Mingle for Singles Ball." She snapped her fingers. "Got to keep the momentum and build excitement for our ball. Nope. We're definitely keeping that. It's a good segue."

Selena avoided Trent's gaze. She reread the letter and jotted down some notes.

Trent reached over to give her hand a squeeze. "You've got this."

She pulled her hand away, feeling uncharitable. He's not the one who would have to lie on air. Tell someone not to do what she herself was doing. Only difference was she was not in love and neither was Trent. But things could get sticky when their fun time was over, and she was already dreading the end.

Carla briefed them on their advertisers and sponsors, and who they needed to mention and not mention. Selena tuned her out; her guilt took precedence. She really didn't want to tackle this subject on the air.

Her cell buzzed. Trent had sent her a message.

It's not the same.

She cut her eyes at him. He sent another.

They are not us.

And another.

We have an understanding.

Pursing her lips, she tossed her phone into her bag. Nothing he had to say was helping. But then it occurred to Selena that because she was in this *weird*ship with Trent, she was the perfect person to advise this man to avoid entanglements at work. Yeah, that's right. She was giving the very advice she needed to take. Not that she would. Or wanted to. But the *sex*tanglement with Trent wouldn't lead to tears because they were friends. They knew what they were doing and could stop this arrangement at any time.

Selena straightened. She felt much better. Once she had settled that in her mind—or as therapist in her would say, "rationalized her actions"—Selena felt excitement to launch their show. The publicity team had provided uploaded photos, redone their slogan, and created a jingle for their segment. And her new hair and makeup team and stylist had her looking amazing. Talk about an upgrade.

Selena's curls had been tamed and she wore a banana-yellow suit with a white shirt, accessories and brown pumps. They had chosen a bronze palette for her face and chocolate for her lips. She looked sultry but expert. Nailed it.

Hotness personified.

Trent strove to keep his eyes off Selena. Or rather, keep from looking at her *that* way. Like he wanted to lick that chocolate off her mouth and investigate what was hidden under that suit tailored to her body. A body he had gotten to know intimately from head to toe. The knowledge was both satisfying and torturous. Because his hands, his lips, his mouth knew and was using this moment to remind him.

But he couldn't give anything away with a glance or a tad-too-personal touch. So he did what he could, which was to utter a paltry, "You look nice," and kept it moving. When Carla gave the cue, Trent began, "Welcome to *Weeknights with Trent and Selena* at our new time. We are happy to be back and to give you an extra hour of enjoyment." After giving the usual weather and major news update, with him and Selena bantering back and forth, he said, "Well, you know the drill. Let's get right to it. It's time for us to *Listen to Our Listeners.*"

Selena leaned into the microphone. "Tonight, we

have a letter from a man who has dubbed himself, 'Wounded at Work.'" Clearing her throat, she read,

"'My company has a strict policy against office romances. I know because I am the human resources officer. But the first day she walked into my office, I was entranced. I had to be around her. I had to be in her presence. It took a minute, but soon we became friends and eventually she welcomed my advances. We dated under the radar. Everything was going well until we got a new CEO. She dumped me and now they are together. But I can't do or say anything, and I'm mortified. And heartbroken. I don't know how much longer I can take seeing her every day because now we aren't even friends. Yet, seeing her makes my day. In that regard, I have no regrets. What do I do?'"

When Selena finished, Trent spoke up. "Whoa. Sounds like this brother is really suffering. It reminds me of the saying, 'It's better to have loved and lost than not to have loved at all.' Why don't you call in with your thoughts while we hear what Selena has to say?"

He settled into his chair, trying to appear relaxed. But he was shaken. Shaken at some of the similarities with his current situation and this dude. Shaken at the thought of losing Selena's friendship if things between them went sideways. He wiped his brow with a paper towel, feeling the high beam of the light shining on him like it would reveal his own truth.

She cleared her throat. "Sometimes the heart wants what it wants, so I do understand how you're feeling. On one hand, you were both adults and it was consensual, so there's not much to say on that. But in this case, you violated work policy. I think your wise option is to learn from your mistake and move on. There must be other positions elsewhere that would welcome someone with your skills. Wounded at Work, I think it is time you moved on so you can smile again."

For a split second, Trent lost his words. He heard words like *mistake* and *move on* and his heart bellowed at him to protest, to tell Selena that they wouldn't end like that. That their end would be amicable. That they would always be friends. That she was his one and only work affair. She was his exception.

Selena flashed him a daring look and asked, "So, Trent, what's your opinion?"

His heart hammered out any rational thought. "I, uh, think I'm going to remain impartial on this one... I think..." Lights flashed and he had to swallow the panic and redirect. "I think we need to get what others have to say." He pressed one of the buttons.

"Listen, you guys are starting off tonight with a banging topic. This man needs to stop whining. You had a taste and it was good. Pat yourself on the back that she didn't come after your job," the caller said.

Trent gave a small noncommittal chuckle. "Thanks for sharing your opinion."

"Dude is just mad because she got an upgrade. Girlfriend is looking out for her interests and if you ask me, he took advantage of her. Maybe she didn't think she could say no…"

His brows shot up and he swung his gaze Selena's way. "I would hate if that were the case. Because I'm all about a woman's choice. I hope you're wrong and she didn't feel pressured or like she had to accept his proposition." He wiped his sudden sweaty palms on his jeans. This topic was more than he'd bargained, making him think about things he hadn't previously considered.

With a light shake of the head that he hoped was meant to reassure him, Selena interjected, "I get the impression that this isn't a damsel in distress situation. I agree with Trent and I do think she made the choice to get involved because it felt right at the time. And then when it didn't…" She shrugged and trailed off.

Trent almost lost his breath. Was Selena saying she was losing interest already? "Hearing these comments is making me feel sorry for Wounded at Work. Call me romantic, but I think this man felt something genuine and he took a chance. A chance at something good. I can't fault him for that. In fact, I think it was brave."

His cohost gave him a tender smile and his heart

relaxed. The rest of the calls were a mixed bag, lightening the atmosphere.

One woman said, "I wanted to ask if you could give Wounded at Work my number since he's now single. I think home girl missed out on a good man and I have no problem scooping him up."

And even another made him laugh. "Since Wounded's available, let him know I own my own business and he can come work for me both on and off the clock."

"It doesn't look like Wounded is going to be alone for long," Selena said with a giggle. "Especially since we are offering him VIP access to our Valentine's Mingle for Singles Ball. Wounded, make sure to call in so we know where to send your ticket. All expenses paid."

Carla cut to the commercials and also plugged the Valentine's Ball. His producer had been right. This topic was a winner, so they kept with it for the rest of the show. Their social media feeds blew up. Men and women were sharing their tales using the hashtag Wounded with their location. And, many were asking Wounded at Work to post his picture.

To top off the night, Wounded actually called in. His voice sounded like that of a radio announcer, which drove everyone wild.

When he sent his picture in, Selena's eyes widened. Then she teased, "Ladies, I can testify that Wounded has a face and body to match that voice. Put it this way, he does not look like a human resources officer. More like a bodyguard. If we could post this picture, he would break the internet."

Trent snatched the photo out of her hand. He was tall, bulky, and had a crooked nose, which told that he had been in a fight or two, so the man could handle himself. If Trent were less confident, he would be jealous at how Selena gushed over him. But Trent didn't have any hang-ups.

"He's all right, fellas. Some of you still got a chance so sign up on our website for an opportunity to win tickets, because this event just got even hotter. It is going to be the Valentine's Day event of the year."

Before they signed off, Selena did her usual call for A Crying Heart to reach out.

Once Carla called cut and the room had cleared, Trent cornered Selena to confront the issue most on his mind. "Do you feel in any way pressured to be in this with me? I don't want you think I'm taking advantage of you."

Her mouth dropped. "You're really asking me that?"

He nodded.

She crooked her finger and led him into her dressing room. Then she slammed the door and turned the lock.

"Someone could see or hear us," Trent said, seeing the wicked intent in her eyes.

Selena pushed at him, causing him to back up until he fell onto the couch. Then she straddled him.

"You must have forgotten who kissed whom first."
She took off her jacket. "You must have forgotten
who straddled you in the cab." She pulled the tank
over her head. "And you must have forgotten when
I said I was ready."

Relief seeped through him. His arms snaked
around her waist. "I remember now," he breathed,
his body heating at her words.

She lowered her head. "Just in case, you don't remember it all, let me remind you." Then she kissed
him, doing unmentionable, wonderful things, driv-
ing him to the edge, showing him just who was in
charge this night.

Chapter Twenty

Things were falling apart. Selena sat in the conference room, peeking out the window, trying to ignore the man sitting beside her. Everything had been going great, both personally and professionally. The ratings grew daily. Trent had her screaming with passion and she returned the favor almost nightly. But then Carla had called a meeting and her announcement became the pin that pierced the happy balloon.

Selena and Trent had arrived in separate cabs even though they had spent most of the day in bed once Pammie had left for school. Especially since Pammie had gone to her cooking class once school let out.

It had starting snowing that afternoon and the forecast predicted an accumulation of about eight inches. However, almost nothing closed the city or showbiz, so she had pulled on her snow boots and headed into work.

Carla plopped beside her hard enough to cause the leather chair to spin on its wheels. Steadying herself, she took a deep breath, exhaled, and dropped the news. "We lost the venue. A major celebrity couple—possibly Beyonce and Jay-Z—have secured the Gotham Hall for an exclusive bash."

Trent jumped to his feet and placed his hands on his hips. "That's some straight-up nonsense right there. Please tell me you're joking."

All Carla could do was shake her head.

Selena's mouth dropped. "How? We signed a contract and paid the deposit."

Carla's gaze shifted. "It turns out our finance department had some snafu and didn't give the final sign-off."

"Are you serious?"

Trent released a long breath. "This is a mess. We have all these people hyped to come and nowhere to put them." He threw his hands up. "Our reputations are going to be like wet bread. What are we going to do?"

"For one thing, we have to keep calm." Carla waved a hand. "We can fix this. I've got some of our best interns scouting out another place."

Selena's brows furrowed. "But the Gotham Hall was perfect. And Valentine's Day is right around the corner. We can't end up in the boondocks. Not when we promised our listeners a grand affair." She placed her head in her hands and sighed. "This cannot be happening."

"It's a PR nightmare," Trent huffed. "There's no guarantee we'll find a suitable place to back up all that talking we've been doing."

Carla tried again. "Let's keep positive."

"It's our faces in the limelight, our names are going to be smeared," Trent shot back, pointing his finger to his chest. He paced the room. "I could ask the shelter…"

Carla straightened. "It's not going down like that. Leave it to me." Her gaze darted between them. She leaned forward and clasped her hands in a tent. "Guys, I have other information to share that I need you to know before you go on this evening."

Something in her tone made Selena's stomach tighten. Her first thought was that Carla had heard about their hookups, and her heartbeat went into overdrive. She flashed a glance at Trent, whose eyes were pinned on hers. His brows rose, a signal and warning for her to remain cool. That would be impossible because she was already sweating through her silk blouse. He shook his head and returned to sit beside her. Selena tried to think of what she would say if Carla confronted them.

"What's going on?" Trent said, appearing unconcerned.

"It has come to our attention that A Crying Heart is no longer with us. She decided to end her life."

Trent's eyes popped in disbelief. "When?"

"Yesterday," Carla whispered in a solemn tone. "We received a letter from her last night."

Selena clutched her stomach, trying to contain her shock. There were so many hurting people out there and they lacked the skills to navigate their pain. Yet she had closed her practice. Selena felt the weight of that choice, though, rationally, she knew she was one woman and could only reach so many. But now she was one less ear for the hurting. That still had impact.

"Where's the letter?" she asked, drawing deep breaths.

"It's in my office." Carla turned to her; eyes filled with compassion. "I know this is gut-wrenching. A Crying Heart's— No. Let me pay her the proper respect by saying her name. Her name was Daphne. Daphne Young. And her letter was the impetus that led to the Valentine's Ball, the boost in ratings…"

"Our show's added success." Trent rubbed his head and exhaled. "Our listeners are going to be distraught when we drop the news tonight."

Carla shifted and cleared her throat. "We're not. I spoke with the board and they advised against it. News like this could bring a damper, stop the impetus and add a bad note to your new show. Our folks did some digging and Daphne was destitute."

Trent shook his head. "So the real concern is they are worried about the potential loss in ratings…" He released a sigh filled with disgust. "Daphne was a human being. Maybe hearing about her demise might lead others to seek assistance."

Selena had to interject. "Or it could drive them into a deeper depression. Lead to copycats…"

"That's a valid point," Carla said.

Trent faced her. "You agree with them?"

"No, but I have to present the other side, the full picture, because that is a very real possibility."

Daphne Young's death made Selena think of Helen. She was grateful someone had been there to intervene or her mother could be gone. Selena checked in with the facility for updates on Helen's progress and was dedicated to honoring the woman who'd brought her into the world by ensuring Helen had first-class care. But Selena hadn't visited, not wanting to cause a setback, face rejection or to be cussed out again. After today though, Selena vowed to reach out to Helen. Try once more to build a relationship.

"News like this won't remain hidden for long." Trent clenched his jaw. "I won't go on the air and keep asking for her to show up when I know the truth."

"I'm not asking you to do that," Carla snapped. "I was more saying to stop asking for her. Focus on the dance." She did a jig in the chair. "Keep things happy and light, at least until Valentine's Day. We can prepare a special memorial for her that we share at the end of the ball."

Selena lifted a hand. "I don't think that's the way

to go. I agree with Trent. If it does come out that she died, Trent and I will look heartless and superficial, and that's not even close to who we are. You said she was destitute. How about we offer to pay her funeral costs? How about we honor her by giving her a proper send-off?"

Trent eyed her with respect. "Now that is a plan that makes sense."

Carla's eyes lit up. "Yes. That's a much better and palatable idea. Let me run it by the board. I'll let you know next steps once I've cleared it with them." She gathered her personal items and headed toward the door. As she walked, she mumbled to herself, "Maybe we can reach out to her family... send flowers..."

Once they were alone, Trent glanced upward. "You know I thought she had found out about us."

"Yes, I was really scared there for a minute. But I would prefer that over learning someone had taken their own life." Selena was dreading the conversation with their listeners. She prayed she could help them and not fall apart herself.

"Are you going to be okay talking about this with everything going on with your mom?"

"How did you know I was thinking of her?"

He gave a look of tenderness and came around the room to sit next to her. "I care about you. You have no idea how much I check you out on the down-low. I enjoy watching you, learning your expressions. So, yes, I knew the exact moment when you thought of Helen."

Her chest heaved. "You watch me?"

"All the time." He held up a hand. "I know that sounds weird, but you're the cutest while you sleep. You make these little sighs that drive me wild. Your lips curl into a smile all the time and I wonder who or what you're dreaming about." He touched her curls. "You're the most exciting woman I have ever been involved with."

Whew. His words drew her in. She lowered her eyes. Her lashes grazed her cheeks. "You're really expecting me to believe that?"

Tucking his finger under her chin, Trent tilted her head back. "It's the truth. I want to be the one who makes you smile that secret smile at night, and I know we're both not looking for anything long-term, but I care about you. That's why you're going to let me lead the announcement and discussion involving Daphne's death during the broadcast. You can do the intro, weather and news, and then hand it over to me."

"I…" She was glad for his help, but she didn't want to be viewed as weak and in need of rescuing. It was a delicate balance. But once again, Trent had interpreted her thoughts with precise accuracy.

Trent stood and loomed over her. "Selena, you're strong, I'll give you that. You had crappy parents and yet somehow all that crap became a fertilizer boosting your growth. Despite your thorns, there's no mistaking that you've become an exquisite rose." He held out his hand. "Let me help you."

Her breath caught and the air tightened with desire at those words. Since she couldn't act on her impulses, she arched a brow and sought to lighten the mood. "So, I have thorns?" Ignoring his hand, she got to her feet.

He smirked. "I took time to craft that sentiment and that's what you hear? When I'm not watching you, that's what I do. I try to think of ways to express what I'm feeling."

She cracked up and placed her hand in his, and they walked out of the room. "I'll demonstrate just how much I appreciate your effort later." She paused. "Wait—no. Let me say it how you would: Your flattery is as smooth as peanut butter on bread, and I plan to spread some on you later."

He looked around before daring to brush his lips against hers. "Looking forward to it." It was short, quick, but it made her lose her equilibrium. Selena would have stumbled if he hadn't grabbed her. "Quit falling for me," he teased.

Selena chuckled and winked at him but, on the inside, she quivered. How could one stop falling if one was already in an undignified heap on the ground? The solution came quickly. Simply not fall. That was good because she absolutely wouldn't. Love was like a dandelion blowing in the wind until only a shell of the former flower was left.

* * *

"Hold still." He released a long whoosh of breath from his position between her legs as she lay on her back. It was the morning after they had shared the news of Daphne's passing with their listeners. Condolences had flooded their page with many encouraging each other to get help if needed. Trent and Selena hadn't wanted to be alone so he had followed her home and had ended up spending the night since he had agreed for Pammie to attend her first sleepover.

"I can't. I can't take it." Her body shook as she gripped the sheets. He watched her stomach muscles contract from her laughter. "I don't know why I let you talk me into this."

"I'm almost done." Trent, at the edge of Selena's bed, as naked as when he'd entered the world, was holding her left foot in one hand and a bottle of tangerine polish in the other. He dipped the tiny brush into the bottle before applying the polish onto her smallest toe.

She kicked and, if he hadn't maintained a firm grip, Trent was sure he would be nursing a bruise on his face. "I had no idea you were so ticklish."

Snickering, Selena said, "See, that's why I hardly ever get pedicures. I can't control myself. It's embarrassing for a grown woman to laugh uncontrollably over getting her feet done."

"I think it's cute."

"You think everything I do is cute."

"That's true." Trent couldn't argue there. He complimented her often when they were together. For some reason, his mouth seemed to come to life around her. When he wasn't kissing her, he was spouting flowery sentiments. Now, Trent had never been the type to flatter, so he found his actions nauseating. But he couldn't stop himself.

Everything about her—her hair, her body, her attitude, and especially her sharp mind—fascinated him. He had never met anyone he considered his equal before Selena. Yet she was in every way that mattered. Plus, Pammie adored her.

If he were the marrying type, he— Whoa. Marriage? Trent almost dropped the polish on her cream-colored sheets. That word had no business invading his thoughts. Besides, love preceded marriage and, though he had love for Selena, it wasn't the kind where he knew he couldn't do without her. Because if she ended their fun times tomorrow, he wouldn't have a problem moving down a level to the just-friends stage.

Trent finished Selena's other foot and then commanded she lie still until her toes dried. Of course, he didn't make it easy by kissing her legs and making his way upward. By the time he was done, they were engaging in another lovemaking session.

As they lay wrapped in each other's arms, both their cell phones went off at the same time. Trent stretched across the bed to get his phone. He scanned the text and groaned.

Selena yawned. "Who is it?"

"It's Carla, and she wants to see us. We have an hour."

Propping up on her elbows, Selena retrieved her cell phone from her bag at the side of the bed, exposing the top half of her body to his feasting eyes. She wrinkled her nose once she had read the text message. "What do you think is going on now? I can't take any more bad news about this event."

"It must be something big if she gave us a time frame." Trent stood and dug around the bed for the rest of his clothes. He found his jeans. His sweatshirt and underwear's location were a mystery.

His cohost's eyes went large. "That's a good point. I didn't think of that." She tossed the covers to the side and slipped out of bed. "I've got to get showered." Stifling another yawn, she said, "I hope it's quick, so I can get some more sleep before our show. Plus, I have to stop by the facility. I'm going to see my mother."

He traipsed to her side and touched her arm. "Do you need me to come with you?"

"No, they're only giving me fifteen minutes, so I should be fine."

"Okay. If you change your mind…" His feet touched a piece of fabric. He bent down to investigate and then chuckled. Trent picked up the bundle and held it for Selena to see. "Now I know where our underwear went."

Selena covered her mouth. "When did that get

here?" She snatched it out of his hands and tossed it into her hamper before going for clean underwear. "If you open the last drawer in the chest, you will see some boxer briefs."

"You got them for me?"

"No. I bought them for a hobo in the train station. Of course, I got them for you."

He paused. "I didn't realize we were at the spare-clothes-in-a-drawer stage."

"As much time as you spend here? I have one of your sweaters, and I washed it. You can wear that." She spun away from him and headed to her walk-in shower.

He followed her, acutely aware of how domesticated this seemed. The spare drawer had spiked his heart rate. A sudden urge to retreat home to shower and put some space between them overtook him. Trent exhaled. Maybe he needed to ease up with the compliments. His smooth talking might lull Selena into thinking they were more than a season.

She had already shoved her hair under a shower cap and was pressing on the Dove bottle to get some soap on her lather builder.

He got a grip on his panic and stepped under the hot spray, moving close to her. Before he could broach the topic of their understanding, Selena addressed him in a gruff tone. "I wore your sweater home the other day. So I washed it. It's not a big deal."

Pumping some of the soap on a washcloth he'd

left hanging the last time he was at her place, Trent said, "I know."

"You think I didn't see your face when I said that? Your fear was very apparent."

He swallowed; unaware he had been that transparent. "I didn't expect to hear that you had bought me underwear. It caught me off guard." He scooted nearer and she stiffened, prickly. Her thorns were out.

"Whatever. You don't have to wear the briefs. I'll take them back and you can go bare. If you scrape your penis on the zipper of your jeans, that's your business." She rinsed off and stomped out of the stall. Grabbing one of the large towels, she dried herself in a hurry, like she couldn't wait to get out of his presence.

He winced at her words and finished washing himself. "Thank you for being thoughtful and for thinking of me. I overreacted."

Her eyebrow arched. "You're welcome." She wrapped a towel about her. "I fought my way through a lot to become an independent woman. I like my space. I like my job. And for the most part, except for when you put your foot in your mouth, I even like you. But don't get it twisted. I'm not secretly pining for a relationship. Not for one millisecond do I believe you're willing to give more than you already have. I know that and, when it comes to anything long-term with you, my expectations are low and my eyes are wide open." Then, with a curl of the lip, she gave him the once-over, dropped her towel and sailed out of the room, her head held high.

Well, dang. Talk about dropping the mic, or in this case, the towel. She had told him about himself.

Goose bumps had sprinkled his arms and chest at her frigid words. He turned off the shower and stepped out. He fumed, churning on her words. So she thought he was incapable of having anything meaningful with a woman? He was. This lifestyle was by choice.

And fear.

He shoved that admission aside. Drying off, Trent walked out, displaying all this glory. She was already fully dressed in a pair of black corduroy pants and a shimmery sweater, and tapping on her phone. He bent over to get the boxer briefs from the bottom drawer and put them on.

She slid a glance his way and cracked up. "If you need an ego boost, your body is banging. That's why we've been rolling in the sheets."

He shoved his legs into his jeans. The sweater she had left hanging on the side of the bed smelled like ocean and summer breeze when he yanked it over his head. "I'm more than muscle and your go-to for an orgasm on demand."

"What does it matter if you are more? That's all I need." Another mic drop. The woman was positively infuriating. And she was making him feel... used. Like he didn't give her laughs and sharp communication.

Grabbing her purse, she tossed her next words over her shoulder. "Lock up on your way out. My cab will be here in five minutes."

Chapter Twenty-One

Selena chose the same seat she was in the last time she had been in the producers' conference room. Trent rushed in and sat beside her, his shoulder touching hers. She bit her inner cheek to keep from laughing and kept her eyes glued to her phone. He was making sure she acknowledged him and she understood his need to after her cutting words.

He must have stopped by his office to put on some cologne because he was smelling good too, but she couldn't give him the satisfaction of knowing he did get to her. On all levels.

Not that ignoring him was easy. In fact, Trent was impossible to ignore.

He checked all her boxes. His body was delightful, a masterpiece. But it was his brain that truly turned her on. His intelligence was an aphrodisiac. Talking to him had become an addiction she had to feed daily.

That scared her.

Because her heart was stubborn and refused to listen to reason. Her words to Trent about not expecting more had been made in self-defense. Because she didn't want him ending things. So she'd had to pretend like it didn't matter if he stayed.

"I got something for you," he whispered under his breath, snapping her out of her musings.

"What is it?"

"It's in my dressing room."

Her lips quirked. "Really? I thought we agreed no more make-out sessions at work. It's too risky."

He straightened. "That was your idea. I don't care if anyone knows we kicking it."

"I do." She didn't want any pitiful looks when Trent moved on to his next temporary fling. And she didn't want to be seen as one of the proverbial notches on his belt.

Just then, Carla sauntered in, wearing a sweat suit as she was supposed to be leaving on vacation. Selena gasped when she saw the CEO trailing behind. Josephine was dressed in a smart white pantsuit and a burgundy tank. Selena tucked her legs under the chair. Whatever this meeting was about had to be serious. Her stomach muscles tensed.

Carla sat across from them, Josephine by her side. A united front.

Josephine didn't hesitate. She dropped a photo in the center of the table. "Care to explain this?"

Trent reached over to slide it closer so they could see. He picked up the picture and held it at various angles before dropping it next to her. "This is us." His tone was final, certain.

Selena frowned and took a close look. Some of it was blurry but she saw a coat she recognized and a man's head burrowed into her chest. Her heart sank. That was her and Trent in the back of the Town Car.

If she could just be a wet noodle and slide underneath the table... Her face felt hot and she was beyond mortified. Selena couldn't look Josephine in the eyes. "I thought the windows were tinted."

"Obviously not dark enough. Or the light was on," Trent said.

"A contact of mine at the news mag dropped this off to my attention," Josephine said. "Someone sent it to them, asking twenty thousand dollars for the photo. They paid him but, as a favor to me, decided not to print it."

Selena covered her mouth and shook her head. Her reputation, which she had taken years to cultivate, would be shredded in minutes. "I can't believe this is happening."

Trent formed a steeple with his hands. "I'll repay them the money. Are they sure this is the only one?"

Josephine nodded. "I was assured it was."

Carla finally spoke up. She slapped a hand on the table. "I know this is awkward, but are you two an item? Because we can put a spin on things. A couple finding love and hosting a show together. People like that."

"No. We're…we're…" Selena shook her head. She didn't know what they were. She couldn't say she was just messing around with Trent because that would make her appear flimsy. But Trent obviously could.

"We're not ready for any long-term commitment. We got carried away one night. That's all. It was all in good fun." He sounded polish, composed. And he would, because he was used to this kind of fluid flirtation.

She curled her fists to keep from lashing out and blaming him for this mess. Because she had been a willing accomplice in this f-u-n. She slid her gaze to that photo. A very willing accomplice.

"Well, that could be a PR nightmare. We're building a brand here and this move was not the way to go."

F-u-n.

Tears pooled her eyes. Selena sniffled. "I know how this looks. I'm the professional advice giver who's hooking up with the ladies' man."

Trent spoke up. "It wasn't like that."

She swung to face him. "Your face is hidden but you can tell it's me in that picture. I'm straddling you in the back of a cab." She covered her face. "Oh, God help me. I'm ruined. I can't keep doing the show. I'm a hypocrite."

Josephine held up a hand. "Easy. This has already been quashed. The station does not have a policy against office entanglements, but we do think it's unwise to have a dalliance with someone you work with. I hope you take that under advisement." The CEO excused herself.

Carla clicked her tongue and jabbed her index finger on the table. "This thing between you two had better not mess up my show."

As soon as she was gone, Trent said, "Well, that went well."

Selena released a plume of air. "Please, now is not the time for sarcasm, because I'm beyond humiliated."

He glared. "We're grown. It's nobody's business what we do when we leave this place."

"Don't you feel any way about that picture? Because, for me, it was a wake-up call."

"I don't feel ashamed for wanting a desirable woman." He eyed her warily. "What do you mean by 'wake-up call'?"

"I'm done with this not-happening relationship. We both know it's not going anywhere anyway, so what's the point. Might as well press the pause button now."

Trent studied her, his jaw clenching, then he jumped to his feet. "All right, if that's what you want." He snapped his fingers. "Consider it done. I've got to get dressed for our show later." He ambled out of the room like her true worth to him was minimal. For him, the end was that easy.

That was the hardest thing he had done in a long time. Thank goodness, Selena hadn't been able to see his face when he'd walked out of the conference room. Trent didn't know how he was expected to sit across from her forty-five minutes from now and smile when it felt like his heart was being peeled like a banana. He felt raw. Exposed.

The worst part was that she hadn't protested. Because he was expendable. Trent shuffled into his dressing room and shut the door. His eyes fell on the gift bag, the tissue hiding the Cargo Birkin inside. A classy gift for a classy woman. But as fast as a finger-snap, it was over. The bag he could return, but the woman he would be working with for years. Years.

Deflated, his shoulders sagged and he slid to the floor, his back against his door. Glancing at his watch, he deduced it had been about four minutes since they'd called it quits. Four minutes. His chest felt inflamed, like a volcano on the verge of erupting from the inside.

Mr. Ejaculate and Evacuate had deviated from his norm and now he was sitting on the floor in his dressing room like a chump. The epitome of a sad love song.

A sharp sting made him clutch his chest. Nah, man. This wasn't about Selena. His heart started racing and he broke out into a sweat. Trent staggered to his feet, huffing with short staccato breaths.

Grabbing his cell, he called James. "Bruh, I think I'm having a heart attack."

"What? Where are you? What happened?" James yelled, sounding panicked. "Did you call 9-1-1?" He fired off the questions.

His chest tightened. "Not yet. But if I don't make it, I need you to pick up Pammie for me. She was at a sleepover and I'm supposed to meet with her friend's parents outside the school at 8:00 p.m."

"All right, I got it. Now, hang up and call 9-1-1, you buffoon. I'm on my way over there."

Trent squeezed his eyes shut, struggling to catch his breath. He heard a slight commotion and then Nadine came on the line. "Wait, let me try something first. What's going on?"

"I feel clammy and my heart is beating faster than a mugger on the run."

"Okay. I need you to close your eyes and take some deep breaths." Her voice was calm and steady.

Trent obeyed.

"Breathe in slowly and breathe out."

He followed her directions.

"Do it again."

After following her instructions, Trent's heart calmed. "It's working. It's working."

"I think you might be having a panic attack. The fact that you were able to carry on a coherent conversation made me think so."

He continued breathing in and out. "Maybe you're right."

"You still should go to the ER and get your vitals checked," she advised. "Did something happen right before you felt this way?"

"Well, Selena and I decided to part ways—not professionally." He cleared his throat. "We're cutting off our extracurricular activities."

Of course, James had heard every word. He broke in the conversation. "Dude, that's what had you all laid out, stressing out a brother by ringing a false alarm. You feeling it because you let a good woman go."

Trent jumped on the defensive. "N-no. That's not it." His brows furrowed. "Maybe it was something I ate."

"It wasn't. You a punk because you done fell in love and you can't handle it. Admit it." James continued to ramble but Trent hadn't heard another word. Though he thought he heard Nadine snickering.

He slapped his forehead. He wouldn't live this down. And Nadine was probably texting Selena about this while they spoke. "I don't do love. Or relationships. And this was a case of indigestion. In fact, I'm pretty sure it's the stromboli I had yesterday."

James now sounded considerably calmer. "If that's what you want to tell yourself. Keep swimming in that lake. See where it gets you."

"What lake?"

"Denial."

Both James and Nadine fell out after that.

Trent rolled his eyes. "That ain't cool, bruh. You didn't feel how I was feeling."

"I was scared out of my mind when you called. But now I know you're okay, it's on, bruh."

"Whatever. I've got a show to do." Trent cut the call just as there was a rap on the door. It was Selena.

"Can we talk?" she asked.

Trent moved aside for her to enter. When he faced her, he took in her calm expression. Nothing about her demeanor indicated that she was feeling the effects of their decision. She looked well put together while he was falling apart. He gathered his pride and squared his shoulders. "What's up?"

A thought occurred. Trent hoped she hadn't come here to gloat about his reaction to their breakup because Nadine would have probably filled her in by now. But she was…normal.

"I just want to make sure things won't be awkward between us." Her eyes slid to the gift bag and he groaned on the inside. Great. This would be a good time for a power surge or crack of thunder. Some kind of diversion to temper his humiliation.

"I'm not about to act the fool and mess up a good thing," Trent said. "We're both capable of maintaining our professionalism."

Her eyes searched his. She touched his cheek. "It was good while it lasted, wasn't it? We had a good run, but this is for the best."

The finality in her tone made him realize that a

part of him must have had a small measure of hope that they would cave and fall back into their arrangement. But her words had crushed it mercilessly and Trent was left feeling ravaged.

Only to himself would he admit that he wasn't going to get past this encounter anytime soon. Selena had made it clear that she thought he was all about the chase and that, for her, it had been a sexual adventure. A period in her life she would look back on and possibly regret. Not so for him. Selena Cartwright had changed his heart. But she was quality, of a different caliber. He didn't deserve her.

Seeing she expected an answer, Trent lied to her for the first time. "I agree." To his horror, his voice cracked.

Her eyes filled with concern. She cocked her head. "Nadine told me you had an...episode. I can run the show without you, if you need." Her kindness, her independence, was almost his undoing. And despite his heartache, he admired her strength.

That's why he summoned his willpower and lied to her a second time. "I'm good. I'll see you out there."

When the door closed beside her, his heart shattered. He felt weak, achy, nauseous, like he could curl up in bed for days. James was right. He was in love. And for Trent, it was every bit of terrible he'd thought it would be.

Chapter Twenty-Two

She had started counting days again.

Ten days before the Valentine's Mingle for Singles Ball, Carla had announced that they had secured the Lotte New York Palace in Midtown. After that declaration, Carla had tossed her Tums into the trash. Both Trent and Selena had rejoiced.

Eight days before the Valentine's Ball, they had secured a deejay and had finally posted the names of the four hundred winners on their website.

And, now she only had five days until the Valentine's dance. Five days until she would campaign for her own show. A morning show. And she was ready. Ready to stop seeing those eyes, smelling that cologne and wanting a taste of the man seated across from her almost every day of the week. Ready to hand in the proposal she carried daily in her bag. The documents were her pacifier, her soothing blanket that gave her the strength to face Trent another day. If her bid for a new show failed, then she would put her big girl panties on and keep wearing her armor of pretense that she was easy-breezy, A-Okay.

For the worse she felt on the inside, the more she made sure she looked her absolute best on the outside. "Break My Stride," a song her mother used to play all the time, was her theme song. She had even played it for Helen during visiting hours now that her mother was back in her room again. Her heart had lifted seeing Helen bop her head to the music. Her mother still didn't speak to her much, but she did say hello and goodbye. When Selena had brought her flowers, her mother had smiled and said, "Thank you." For Selena, civility had to be enough.

She'd just vacated the building when her cell rang. "Hey, Nadine. Did you get the papers?" To fight her heartsickness, Selena had been concentrating on her foundation. She had most of the paperwork completed and Nadine had agreed to be her CEO. After the ball, they would start planning the launch. Selena intended to keep herself so busy that she wouldn't have any energy to think about Trent.

"Yep. I got them notarized on the job. You should get it tomorrow by messenger."

"That is fabulous. Don't forget to clear your schedule so we can scout a couple locations." The wind blew at her hair and Selena burrowed into her coat.

"I already did. You are going to help so many people. I can't wait to be a part of this."

Hearing the other line, Selena checked her screen and saw an unexpected caller. "Nadine, let me call you back in a few."

"Sure thing."

Selena swept her hair out of her face and clicked over. "Pammie? Are you okay?" She pressed the phone to her ear as worry set in, and hailed a cab. When she got in, the driver turned on the meter but she held up a finger.

"Hi, Ms. Selena. I'm okay. Guess what?"

Pammie's upbeat tone put Selena at ease. "Hang on." She gave her address to the cabdriver and then asked, "Okay, I'm back. What's going on?"

"I'm going on a date! Franco is taking me to see a movie." The excitement in her voice was infectious.

Her mouth fell open. Trent must have finally relented and allowed Pammie to go out with the opposite sex. But with Franco? That was nothing short of amazing. "That's wonderful. I'm really happy for you. You've got to tell me how it goes."

She wondered if Trent was in earshot and overhearing this conversation, how he felt about it. She felt a pang. This was something he would have told her before. But now their relationship was strained off the air. When they worked, the chemistry, the banter, made their ratings continue to rise. But once they were done, Trent was usually the first one out the door, like he couldn't get away from her fast enough. No matter how that hurt, she kept her composure. *Smile and nod,* the Jamaican way.

"Yeah. But I need your help. I don't know what to wear. Can you come over?" Pammie's tone was hopeful.

"I…" Selena paused. She remembered her first date, how her mother wasn't involved and how that had felt. She couldn't disappoint her. "Sure. I'll be right there. See you in a few."

When she entered Trent's building, her heart pounded. Selena approached the penthouse elevators, praying she still had access. Fortunately, the desk clerk recognized her and within a few minutes, she was stepping into Trent's suite.

Pammie stood waiting. The young woman fell into Selena's body and wrapped her arms about Selena's waist. "I missed you." Pammie had taken out her extensions and her natural curls hung on her shoulders. She was wearing a burgundy robe.

Selena patted her on the back. "I missed you, too." Her heart swelled. She didn't realize how much Pammie had come to mean to her in such a short time. Her ears were cocked, listening for Trent, but this place was big enough that he could be in another area.

Seeing Mindy hovering in the background, Selena waved a hand in greeting. Mindy had an apron over her shirt and jeans, and held a kitchen towel in her hand. Judging by wonderful smells, the woman was baking a cake.

Releasing her, Pammie took Selena's hand. "Let's go in my room."

Allowing herself to be led, Selena gasped when she entered Pammie's space. Pammie's bedroom had been given an overhaul. Almost all of her stuffed animals were gone. The walls were now a light shade of gray and had a huge mural with a backdrop of a black ballerina midair. Large letters spelled her name on the wall. She had a new queen-sized bed with a comforter set that was a blend of pink, gray and white. Selena smiled when she noticed a couple unicorns amid the coordinated pillows. Though she was grown, it was good to see Pammie hold on to treasures of her youth.

"Your room is beautiful."

She did a cheerful little jump. "Trent did it. He says I'm older now. And I got to pick out what I want. Plus, look at this." She raced to the bed, lifted the blanket and started to tug at what looked like a large drawer. Selena rushed to help her. "There's another bed here for when I have sleepovers. I've gone to two sleepovers now. One at Rosa's house and another at Emily's."

"I love your bed, Pammie."

"Yeah, Trent says I can take it with me when I get my own place. But I can't get an apartment until I'm at least twenty-five."

Selena hid her smile. She walked over to the closet and opened the door. "Let's decide what you're going to wear. Do you know where you're going?"

Pammie was by her side in a flash. "Yes. We're going to watch a movie and eat popcorn. Ms. Mindy is taking us because Trent went out. But she won't sit where we're sitting. Oh, and Franco says he's paying, but Trent says I need to have my own money just in case."

"Trent is so right about that." She gave the appropriate response but she'd felt a deep puncture in her gut when she'd heard Trent was out. On a date? He couldn't already be seeing someone. Not so soon. She thought about her sleepless nights and drew in a deep breath. Selena touched her abdomen, willing herself to remain calm and to remember she was here for Pammie and not Trent. Selena forced the man from her mind and continued her conversation with Pammie.

"It sounds like it's going to be wonderful." She placed a hand under Pammie's chin. "Let's get you a cute top with some jeans to wear and I'll do your makeup."

Pammie cocked her head. "Do you want to come with us?"

Aww. Her generosity melted Selena's heart. "No, sweetheart. You enjoy your time with Franco. Do you know what you're going to talk about with him while you're on your date?"

She nodded. "Yes, Trent and I practiced conv... conversation, since this is my first date. I wrote down some ideas in my cell phone in case I forget."

The image of Trent helping his sister got her

teary-eyed. He was so sweet and thoughtful with Pammie. She dabbed at her eyes and spent the next hour helping Pammie decide on the right outfit and applying her makeup. When they were done, Selena snapped several pictures with her phone. Just before she left, she made Pammie promise to call her to tell her all about her date.

On her way home, Selena's heart felt light. Seeing Pammie today made her realize her time with Trent had been more meaningful than physical gratification. She was thankful to have played a small role in helping Trent begin to transition Pammie toward independence, and smiled her first genuine smile in days.

His custom gray Berlutti suit had arrived. Trent stood in his closet with only a towel wrapped around his waist, admiring the cut, sure it would be a perfect fit. He planned to wear the suit with a plum-colored shirt, an ode to Valentine's Day. In less than two hours, he needed to report to the Lotte New York Palace to greet the deejay, The Vocalz girl group and the members of the live band. They would have an hour or two to practice and a warm-up before the event officially opened to guests.

The interns were already there to oversee everything and to manage the press and cater to the VIP guests, which included about fifty single celebrities. Trent and Selena had hired drivers and would arrive in black SUVs at a set time for photos and to hype up the event with the press. Selena had selected to wear a plum dress to match his shirt but he wasn't sure if she would choose another, considering…

There he went thinking about Selena again. Not that it was any surprise. Trent thought about her constantly. He had set a goal to try to keep these musings from being an hourly thing to a once-a-day thing until he had exorcised her out of his head and heart. So far, he hadn't been able to achieve that. James and Dontae called it moping, but he chose to see it as contemplation. For example, he contemplated why it felt so good to be in her presence every day at the station. So alive. He contemplated why he couldn't get images of Selena in his bed out of his mind, while he slept in his guest room.

He already knew the reason. Love. Unreciprocated love. He was unequivocally, madly, passionately, in love with Selena Cartwright. And though she didn't feel the same, his heart anticipated seeing her in all her fineness at the ball.

And he wasn't the only one experiencing anticipation.

There had been an unexpected outcome of the Valentine Mingle for Singles Ball. Turned out that when they'd posted the winners and invited them to join a private Facebook group, the singles had started connecting. And connecting. Now many of them were looking to meet and hook up at the dance. A lot of the other stations and TV networks would have a correspondent on what they were calling the Biggest Love Match of the Year.

Selena had tried to redirect the focus of the ball to that of celebrating singlehood when the hashtag LoveMatchDance started trending, but she had been unsuccessful. Over the past couple evenings, that was all their listeners wanted to talk about—who they had met online and what they planned to wear.

Trent, on the other hand, had encouraged it. He wanted to see love work out for other couples, especially since it sucked for him. But at least he had moved up from misery to a constant, dull ache. He understood why they called this emotion a bug. Although, for him, a better metaphor was a tapeworm. Because this love was like an invasive infection that had infiltrated every aspect of his life. He didn't think he would ever recover.

Pammie walked into his closet. "There you are. I was calling you."

He gripped the towel with his hand to keep it secure. "Hey, sis. I'm about to get dressed. What's up?"

"I wanted to give you a hug because Franco called to say he is almost here." She wore a red sheath dress and black shoes. Franco and his parents were taking her out for dinner. This was her second date in a matter of days. Her eyes sparkled and she looked so happy that, even though Trent was ecstatic for her, he felt a touch of envy.

Brushing off that sentiment. "Did you charge your phone?"

She nodded and pointed to his suit. "Is that what you're wearing? Is Ms. Selena going?"

"Yes, I plan to wear this and, yes, Selena will be there with me."

Pammie clapped her hands. "Oh, great. I'm glad you're getting back together."

"Just because we're going together, doesn't mean we're getting back together." Technically, they hadn't ever been a couple but he couldn't tell Pammie about their arrangement. He walked out of the closet and rested the suit on the bed.

Her bottom lip jutted out. "I thought you loved her."

"I do." His chest tightened. That was the first he had admitted out loud how he'd felt about her to anyone. He cleared his throat and uttered the words. "I love Selena a whole lot."

His stomach muscles eased. Wow. Even his heart lightened. He tried it again. "I love her so much that I think about her all the time." Whew. For the first time since he'd made the stunning discovery, Trent felt like he could breathe. He was now convinced. Keeping love bottled up was not the way to go. Love was meant to be expressed. And shared. And experienced.

"I knew it!" Pammie beamed. "If you tell her that, then you will be together forever and ever."

With a sad smile, Trent patted Pammie's shoulder. "I wish it was that simple, but I don't think Selena wants to know how I feel."

Pammie grimaced. "Why not? I'm a girl and I liked it when Franco told me that he liked me."

Whoa. As simple as it sounded, Pammie might have a point. Franco was a brave man. Braver than Trent.

His heart thundered. "But what if I tell her I like her and she doesn't like me back?"

Pammie shrugged. "Then that's okay." She cocked her head. "You just tell someone else. Because if Franco didn't like me, I would just tell Mason that I like him."

He mulled on her words for a beat.

Suddenly, laughter bubbled within him at the simplicity, at the wisdom, in her advice. Trent laughed and laughed. In just a few minutes, Pammie had solved all his angst. "Thanks, little sister. You really are growing up."

"That's what I told you. Because I'm almost twenty-two."

Snatching her close, Trent said, "I love you."

Pammie reached up to pat his head and then gave a dramatic sigh. "I know that already. Tell Ms. Selena. After you put on your clothes."

Chapter Twenty-Three

Selena stood near the entrance of the Villard Ball-room, located on the second floor of the Lotte, and allowed herself a moment to celebrate her and Trent's accomplishment. Four hundred singles of all shapes and sizes mingled in small groups, talking and laughing, having a great time.

The deejay was playing some old jams that had people getting down on the dance floor. There was also plenty of food to go around. She had tasted some of the chicken quesadilla wraps and the buffalo cauliflower wings and they were delicious. Judging by the early reports on social media, the event was a success and a must-do for the following year.

She tucked her Coperni heart-shaped tote under her arm. If the station gave her a show of her own, she could still plan this event next year with Trent. In a year, she would be over him. *Yeah right.*

Enough of thinking about Trent. She was going to have herself a good time.

Selena strolled over to a few of the guests and engaged in small talk.

Her embellished, strapless plum gown fitted her like a sausage casing but she still had room to move because of the light flare at the bottom. And move she did. Selena did the wop, got jiggy with it, and wobbled until her feet hurt. Plus, she took pictures, lots of pictures with her fans.

About an hour in, she heard the deejay announce that Wounded at Work had shown up. All the ladies started screaming and running toward him. Of course, Selena and a couple cameramen went to record the moment and to talk with him since he had quit his job and no qualms about being recognized. Selena thought he looked even better in person and she wasn't the only one. After she interviewed him, he asked her to dance and for her number. Both of which Selena declined, knowing his pants' pockets would be lined with at least a hundred numbers before the night was out.

And that's when she saw Trent standing by the perimeter of the dance floor, holding a clear case in his hand. She thought she had spotted him earlier but he had ventured into the VIP area. She strutted over to him. His gaze was pinned on hers and she stumbled under the intensity. He reached over to steady her so she wouldn't fall. Electricity surged between them and she broke contact before she did something stupid like kiss him.

"I bought you a corsage."

"Why?"

"Because it's a nice thing to do for my cohost." He opened the case. Centered between baby's breath was a plum-colored rose that matched her dress. He slipped it on her wrist.

"Uh, thank you." Figures. Trent was being all sweet right before she broke her news. The gesture made her second-guess her decision. But it was a gesture. She pointed toward a far corner of the room and said above the rising music, "I need to talk to you."

"Good, because I need to talk to you, as well."

They walked to the end of the ballroom. "It's pretty loud in here." He took her hand, pulled her in the direction of the restrooms and entered the women's bathroom. It was a miracle that no one else was inside. There was a sitting room, a separate area for the stalls and washbasins, and a scent diffuser that made the restroom smell of lemon, pomegranate and wood, creating a soothing and sensual atmosphere.

She shook her head. "Where— What are you doing?"

He arched a brow. "You have a better idea?"

"Yes. Anywhere but here. We can just have a conversation like regular people."

"C'mon." Trent chose the largest stall and beckoned her inside. "We can talk in here without fear of being recorded or photographed."

Selena placed a hand on her hip. "Oh, okay. Because it would be so much better to be caught inside a bathroom stall with you. There's no way that could cause a scandal."

His voice dropped. "Just come in and talk to me."

With a sigh, Selena sauntered inside. He reached behind her to lock the stall door, making her acutely aware of the enclosed space. "You are so dramatic. What if someone comes in?"

"No one will see us." He answered with the confidence of a man who had done this before—lock himself in a stall with a woman to do more than talking. But there was no way Selena would ask him about his possible past *sex*cursions.

He cupped her cheeks and she looked at him. His eyes were warm, his expression affectionate. "Now, what do you want to talk about?" He gave her nose a playful tap, which disconcerted her. They'd gone weeks avoiding physical contact with each other and now he was looking at her like he…like he…well, like he liked her. Smiling and teasing. Then he said, "I have something to talk to you about, as well."

Her heart drummed in her chest, reacting to his closeness and his hands. Her body remembered those hands. Her nose, his special fragrance. "What do you have to say?" she whispered.

Trent placed a finger over her lips. "You go first. I don't want to be accused of not being a gentleman." Then he gave her a tender smile that turned her heart into mush.

Slipping the bag off her shoulder, she unzipped it

and took out the letter, her hands shaky. Her lower lip trembled but she drew in a deep breath and made herself voice her intentions. "Trent, I—I wanted to let you know ahead of time that…" She took his hand and squared her shoulders. "I'm planning to pitch my own show. I have an appointment with the board tomorrow."

His eyes bulged and he took a step back. His brow was furrowed, his eyes flashed with feral fury. "But we're a team."

"Yes, but I think this is a great career move for me. I have to do this. I can't bear—"

"Can't bear what?" he asked, voice rising. "Can't bear that you dared to sleep with me?"

She felt her eyes go large; certain they would be overheard if someone entered the bathroom. Panicked, she placed a finger over her lips. "Shh—"

Trent stiffened and puffed his chest. "Don't shush me."

She detected a hint of hurt in his voice and wondered why Trent would take umbrage when he was the one who'd insisted he was a man of just fun.

The outer door creaked, signaling guests had entered the bathroom. Selena looked at Trent and shook her head, silently begging him to remain quiet, not to bring attention to them in the stall. From the sound of things, it was a group of women, talking and laughing, unaware of the turmoil a few feet away from them.

"I'm not ashamed of you," she whispered.

He held up a hand and mouthed for her to wait. They engaged into a stare down until they were once more the only occupants in the restroom.

"I'm not ashamed of you," she repeated. "You won't give me the chance to explain."

He raised his chin. "Maybe you're not ashamed, but you see me as unworthy of you." Trent stepped around her to unlock the door. "I wish you the best, Selena because that's what friends do."

"Yes. We can hang out as friends."

She expected agreement after he had called himself a friend but Trent shook his head and scoffed. "You don't get it, do you?" He looked over her head. "And to think I was going to tell you that I—" He pursed his lips. "You know what, it doesn't matter."

Sudden anger sliced through her. Stuffing the letter in her purse, she stormed after him and snatched his arm, forcing him to turn around. "You know what, it does. I'm a huge romance novel fan, and I hate when things play out like this between the hero and the heroine. I hate when they refuse to speak things out because of a big misunderstanding and I… I can't have that kind of ending. I simply can't have that."

He eyed her with wariness before raising his brow. "What on earth are you rambling about?"

Selena flailed her hands. "Goodness. You're daft." This time her voice escalated but she was past the point of caring. The words spewed out. "I'm in love with you, all right! I can't bear to be around you and not touch you. It's maddening, frustrating, and I can't do it anymore. Here I am celebrating singlehood and bragging how I don't do love, then I go ahead and fall for the first man who gives me an orgasm!" She heard a sharp intake of breath—breaths, actually—behind her, but she pressed on. "You know how pitiful that is?"

Trent's mouth popped open. "Selena, I—I didn't know." Everything about his tone suggested that her confession had caught him off guard. Then his lips quirked. "Wait. I gave you your first orgasm?"

Her bravado deflated. "I just told you that I love you and that's what you hear?" She was sure her face flamed from her mortification. Throwing her arms up in the air, Selena turned around to see the girl group, The Vocalz, standing there, looking gorgeous in their leopard cat suits, eyes filled with pity and mirth.

Cupping her mouth with her hand, Selena raced from the bathroom intending to stuff her face with appetizers.

Carla came over to where she stood. "I heard you're meeting with the board tomorrow," she said, sounding slightly inebriated. "Good luck."

"It's in the bag," Selena said, giving the other woman a high five before returning to the dance floor.

Of all the dumb, muleheaded moves he had ever made, Trent knew his response had been the worst of his sorry life. When Selena had told him she loved him, his heart had rejoiced before fear set in. Unnerved, he had opened his mouth and said something stupid, cracking on one of the most monumental moments in a woman's life. But then he'd had to watch as Selena's face had crumbled.

Trent had been about to fix his egregious mistake and run after Selena when The Vocalz blocked his path. They had folded their arms and stood before him in a single line, refusing to let him pass, declaring they were giving Selena time to escape. They'd called him a few scathing four-letter words that made his ears burn until he had been forced to explain his true feelings. Only then would they let him pass.

He dashed out of the restroom, hoping to spot that exquisite dress and those freak-me-now silver sandals. Not seeing her, he released a breath of frustration. Selena was the one who should have heard his declaration of love first, not four fresh-faced strangers—well, five counting Pammie—who sang about an emotion they possibly knew nothing about. To be fair, he hadn't either though. Until Selena.

He called her cell phone but it went straight to voice mail.

She might have left for home already. Squelching his exasperation, Trent hailed a cab and provided Selena's home address.

He couldn't get to her fast enough.

When the cab swerved in front of Selena's home, he settled the tab, holding a huge bouquet of flowers.

He had bought them for triple what the cabbie, who had purchased them for his wife, had paid.

Heedless of the rain that had begun to fall, Trent darted up the steps, pressing on her doorbell. He peered through the windows, seeing darkness inside. Then he lowered his head and groaned. She wasn't there. He called Selena again but once again, got her voice mail.

He wiped the raindrops from his face and then rubbed his hands. Maybe she had stopped by the studio. Trent didn't know if he should wait or head to the radio station. Because of one second of irrational fear, he had lost his chance.

He plodded down the stairs with his hands stuffed in his pockets, intending to go home. He had asked Mindy to stay over, anticipating being in Selena's bed that night, but it appeared that was not meant to be.

Then he heard a voice. "Giving up, are we?"

He swung to face Selena's elderly neighbor. "Excuse me?" he asked.

"You ran up those steps like you had a grand purpose and you're walking down them with your body bent in defeat."

An eloquent description of his embarrassment. "Do you have nothing better to do than spy on your neighbor?"

"Spy?" He stretched the word in way that made Trent think of Laurence Fishburne in *The Matrix*.

Trent quickly apologized.

With a wave of dismissal, the old man folded his arms. "Do you need to get into Selena's place?"

Hope burst in his chest like firecrackers on Independence Day. There was only one reason Trent could think of why the man would ask.

Trent went over to the neighbor's house and jogged up the stairs. "I would love to go and plan a Valentine's Day surprise for the lady."

Sure enough, the old man waved a hand, holding a bronze key. His eyes held a twinkle that made Trent realize the man was a romantic. "She might have changed the locks. But the previous owners gave me a spare key in case of an emergency."

He exhaled. Here was another person who would hear how he felt about Selena before she did. "I would say being able to tell Selena I love her before Valentine's Day ends constitutes an emergency. Wouldn't you?"

Chapter Twenty-Four

The pouring, freezing rain and her drooping curls were the perfect way to end this horrible night. Selena opened the door to her home and dragged the coat soaked heavy from the downpour off her shoulders before hanging it on the rack along with her bag.

She unzipped her dress and stepped out of the designer gown pooled at her feet. She never intended to wear this dress again. It was a reminder of her mortification.

Her deepest rejection.

Clad in only her underwear, Selena turned on the kitchen light and gasped. She wasn't alone. She emitted a loud shriek before her mind registered that she knew the intruder.

"Trent, what are you doing here? And how did you get in?"

"Your neighbor."

"He has a key?"

"Yes, from the previous owners. I'm glad you never changed the locks."

"That's good to know but he shouldn't have let you in because you don't live here." She scoffed. "Wait, let me guess, you charmed him with your tongue. I swear that tongue of yours can make things happen." She froze as the innuendo behind her words sank in.

Trent clamped his lips, appearing to hold in his smile, and came over to where she stood.

Wearily, she shrugged. "I didn't mean it that way." Remembering their last conversation, her anger re-kindled. She spoke through her teeth. "Again I ask, why are you here?"

Reaching out to hold both her hands in his, he said in a somber tone, "I couldn't let the night end without setting things right."

She sighed. "If you came to apologize, I accept your apology. Now go home. It's all good."

"I love you." He spoke the three words and then looked at her, expectant, as if this was her cue to swoon.

His words of love infuriated her. "This is fickle, even for you. I get that you feel bad, but you don't have to say you love me to make me feel better."

Trent's mouth dropped open and his eyes went

wide. "Are you serious, right now?" His voice escalated. "I tell you I love you and you call me fickle? I
thought I was in love before but what I feel for you
is another level." Looking heavenward, he shouted,
"Is this some sick joke? I fall in love for the first time
in my life and this is what I get?"

Selena's gut knotted when the truth hit her core.

He flashed her a look filled with fire.

Selena gave a little laugh. "What a ridiculous
lovesick pair we are."

"Speak for yourself," he muttered. "There's nothing ridiculous about how I feel. But then again, I am
a joke to you."

Selena bit down on her bottom lip and squeezed
the cheeks of her mouth tight. But she couldn't hold
the snicker. She didn't know why her funny bone
had kicked in, but she doubled over with uncontrol-
lable laughter.

Trent eyes turned glacial. "Care to tell me what's
so funny?" His fury was like fire to her sense of
humor.

She hiccupped through her laughter as she tried
to explain. "It's…just we are a sorry pair of main
characters in this romance."

His shoulders relaxed. "Speak for yourself." Trent
smiled, pulling her into his arms. He placed a teaser
of a kiss on the corner of her mouth. "I, for one, know
how to be romantic." He curved her into his body
and called out to her Siri HomePod to play the or-
chestra version of Miley Cyrus's "Wrecking Ball."

The beautiful sound of the violin and other instruments filled the room and she allowed Trent to take the lead as they danced.

Looking into his eyes, she said, "Is this your idea of being romantic?"

They glided across her living area. "No. If I were trying to be romantic, I would say my life lost its color without you in it. I breathe, I think of you. I eat, I think of you. I dream, I think of you. You're the best laugh, the best lover, and the best friend I ever had. You have ruined me for other women and I'm glad about it. These lips, these hands, this mouth, and every other part of me, belongs to you, are only for you, and will be yours if you want them. Always."

She drew short breaths after those words then cleared her throat. "Well, since you're not trying to be romantic, what do you actually plan to say?" The song finished at the same time she ended her question.

He touched her hair and spoke with tenderness. "How about, I love you?"

Her eyes welled and she touched his face. "Good. Because I love you, too."

Trent swept her off her feet and they shared a passionate kiss. A kiss that continued as he walked her into her bedroom and lay her on the bed of flowers. Shedding his clothes, he leaned in and nipped at her ear before he asked, "So, you never answered my question. Did I really give you your first orgasm?"

She shoved at him. "Really? You need an ego

boost right now?" She chuckled in his chest. "Yes. If you must know, you did."

"Do you want another one or three?"

She shivered as her body was already responding with anticipation. "Yes. Yes, I do."

* * * * *

More second chances at love, try these great books from Harlequin Special Edition:

What Happens in the Air
By Michele Dunaway

Valentines For The Rancher
By Kathy Douglass

Their Sweet Coastal Reunion
By Kaylie Newell

Available now!

#2965 FOR THE RANCHER'S BABY

Men of the West • by Stella Bagwell

Maggie Malone traveled to Stone Creek Ranch to celebrate her best friend's wedding—not fall in love herself! But ranch foreman Cordell Hollister is too charming and handsome to resist! When their fling ends with a pregnancy, will a marriage of convenience be enough for the besotted bride-to-be?

#2966 HOMETOWN REUNION

Bravo Family Ties • by Christine Rimmer

Sixteen years ago, Hunter Bartley left town to seek fame and fortune. Now the TV star is back, eager to reconnect with the woman he left behind...and the love he could never forget. But can JoBeth Bravo trust love a second time when she won't leave and he can never stay?

#2967 WINNING HER FORTUNE

The Fortunes of Texas: Hitting the Jackpot • by Heatherly Bell

Alana Searle's plan for one last hurrah before her secret pregnancy is exposed has gone awry! Her winning bachelor-auction date is *not* with one of the straitlaced Maloney brothers but with bad boy Cooper Fortune Maloney himself. What if her unexpected valentine is daddy material after all?

#2968 THE LAWMAN'S SURPRISE

Top Dog Dude Ranch • by Catherine Mann

Charlotte Pace is already overwhelmed with her massive landscaping job and caring for her teenage brother. Having Sheriff Declan Winslow's baby is just *too much*! But Declan isn't ready to let the stubborn, independent beauty forget their fling...nor the future they could have together.

#2969 SECOND TAKE AT LOVE

Small Town Secrets • by Nina Crespo

Widow Myles Alexander wants to renovate and sell his late wife's farmhouse—not be the subject of a Hollywood documentary. But down-to-earth director Holland Ainsley evokes long-buried feelings, and soon he questions everything he thought love could be. Until drama follows her to town, threatening to ruin everything...

#2970 THE BEST MAN'S PROBLEM

The Navarros • by Sera Taíno

Rafael Navarro thrives on routines and control. Until his sister recruits him to help best man Etienne Galois with her upcoming nuptials. Spontaneous and adventurous, Etienne seems custom-made to trigger Rafi's annoyance...and attraction. Can he face his surfacing feelings before their wedding partnership ends in disaster?

HARLEQUIN
PLUS

Try the best multimedia
subscription service for romance
readers like you!

Read, Watch and Play.

Experience the easiest way to get
the romance content you crave.

Start your **FREE TRIAL** at
<u>www.harlequinplus.com/freetrial</u>.